House of Apollo

Maxwell Olin Massa

HOUSE OF APOLLO

Maxwell Olin Massa

Whisk(e)y Tit
VT * NYC

Published in the United States by Whisk(e)y Tit: www.whiskeytit.com. If you wish to use or reproduce all or part of this book for any means, please let the author and publisher know. You're pretty much required to, legally.

ISBN 978-1-7329596-4-4

Library of Congress Control Number: 2019953584

Cover design by Alice Bedard-Voorhees.

Frostispiece by Ivana.

First Whisk(e)y Tit paperback edition.

SELECT PRAISE FOR
HOUSE OF APOLLO

This wonderfully strange, thought-provoking, and hilarious novel defies simple categorization... The funniest book I've read in a long time.

— Beth Castrodale, *Small Press Picks*

A very different, bitterly amusing dystopic take on the U.S. financial culture.

— L. E. Modesitt, Jr. author of the *Saga of Recluce* series

An elegant, many-layered novel... Where else in the many [books] written about dystopian office life can you find original iambic pentameter?

— Steven Hill, former Chief Legal Adviser, NATO HQ

An eccentric dystopian take on the modern Apollo [...] In theory, the novel is quirky and peculiar, but Massa challenges the reader's intellect and feelings until the end. ... a novel that I thought about a lot.

— *Independent Book Review*

For my mother,
who would have loved an author son

PROLOGUE

"Have a seat. Yes, make yourself comfortable... Before we begin, I just want to confirm: is your name spelled with a 'C' or a 'K'?"

"A 'C', sir."

"Very good. Now, tell me about yourself: why did you choose this line of work?"

"Images communicate, sir. I want to be a communicator."

"I see."

"If you can provide the message, I'll get it out there."

"You seem eager about this."

"I am very eager, sir."

"That is good."

✳

"I've been through your portfolio. Technically, it's quite accomplished."

"Thank you, sir. Unity, technique, and form are all critical to me."

"Describe your process."

"I like specifications. When I receive the design document, I don't try to fight against it. Instead, I like to... it's as if I let my mind empty into it, as if the requirements were a mold, and I had to take on their shape."

"And your vision comes from that?"

"Yes, sir."

"What about when you are working on your own?"

"Why would I do that, sir? Without an assignment, there wouldn't be any point."

"It's just another question on my list. I have to ask everyone."

☀

"Well, I'd say that wraps it up! I think you'll be hearing from us... anything further? Final questions, final thoughts?"

"Yes, my contact information has changed. My new number is on my card."

"Say, that's a handsome case!"

"Thank you. I find it keeps them clean."

"What a satisfying click it has too!"

"I like a good, satisfying click."

"Let me see here – yes, we can make these changes."

"Please keep the card; I designed it myself."

"And to my own specifications, I suppose? Somehow, I could tell... I think Longshot will welcome you, young Caleb. You could go far with us."

"I hope to shine like the sun Himself, sir."

1

Caleb was not beautiful at table. Inclined by nature to view food solely as a source of sustenance and not of pleasure, he had developed a series of time-saving procedures to reduce the daily commitment to feeding, none of which was pleasant to behold. The meal arriving, he was wont to pare the larger chunks on his plate down to a small enough size so that they did not present a choking hazard and then simply slurry everything into a uniform, readily-consumable paste, stopping only when the separate nature of no component part was discernible. By this act he saved much time that would otherwise have been wasted on the delicate but superfluous matter of tailoring every bite and weighing how to pace his meal so as to deliver a maximum of flavor. He would then lower his head directly over the now featureless victuals – his face in perfect parallel to the dining surface, the distance between its receiving port and the goods to be delivered narrowed to its minimum – and shovel. He would not actually see most of what he ate, but there was always a great deal of noise, sort of like a parched animal quenching her thirst at a muddy watering hole. It was a very aggressive snorking, though oddly clean as efficiency was also among his desires. Waste bothered him. After the primary process of becoming fed was accomplished, the serving platter needed to be scraped with programmatic ruthlessness so that no scampering scrap remained; he would then lick the utensils to a gleaming, unsanitary finish. Satiated, his shirtfront remained immaculate.

He ate never at home. This seemed the most logical choice as he need expend no time in food prep, which he found tedious, or in cleaning up, which was beneath him, and he liked to keep his kitchenette factory fresh. He was also relatively well-monied and never obliged to break his bread in the company of anyone, so the economic burden of taking breakfast, lunch, and supper in the eatery was noticeable but not crushing to him. It also provided the perfect conditions for engaging in his favorite post-prandial activity to assist the digestion: staring. He would sit before the devastated table and openly ogle whoever came readily to hand: women for their value as objects of his discerning and frustrated lust and men as specimens for study, as he did so wish to improve himself to the point where his own terrible condition of singlehood might be dissolved.

Yesterday, he had been staring at one of the company auditors.

"Ooooh," the internal monologue had run. "Ooooh, yes. She is an optimal one. Most optimal. My eye observes her curves, takes in with readiness the contours of this broad-faced specimen. She clearly gets good nutrition. I see already in her spending patterns a heavy preference for hygiene and fitness-related products and services. Look how the perfect whiteness of that upper set stands out at almost military attention against the inviting, walnut ruddiness of her skin. Does she frequent the appropriate *couture* sites and pepper her correspondence with quotations therefrom derived? Ooooh, yes. I am certain she does. Optimal, indeed."

The auditor had been blithely unaware. She toyed with her handheld and appeared to receive information that was of mixed value, unwelcome but unimportant. Then she frowned with her brow and her lip, finishing with the kiss of a pout. Caleb saw it all. With a directed gesture, she signaled to the kitchen that preparations for her first course could commence. Briefly, dimly, she had seemed conscious of being the object of some sort of social attention, perhaps from the well-dressed gentleman in the tight-fitting slacks, there in the corner? She had looked about nervously and re-crossed her legs. Then she returned her attention to her device and remained buried in consultation of it as Caleb's eyes remained upon her.

"Optimal. A perfect fit," the monologue continued. Caleb was, in fact, a well-dressed man and lavished much of the time saved in nourishing his body on clothing it. His shirt was tailored and his buttons shone. "And a breeding one, too. The indicators are obvious, even from her commercial behavior: look at the brands, the labeling. All of it from the finer shops, but not this season's offerings, and her bag is screaming at its seams that it was last year's hottest pattern. This is a woman who is saving, a woman who plans. And planning is these days, as we well know, strongly correlated with the willingness for children in females. It is the wastrel woman who is wanton, it is she who delights in having those terrible, infant-preventing things implanted – the spend-crazy twenty-nothing. They are sterile. But not you, dear thing." He had adjusted a cuff to display the warmth of his tan to greater effect, for he was toned all over to the burnish of a coffee diamond. "This woman's data, her patterns," he smoothly mused, "delight." At this point, dwelling on the potentials of the young employee's browsing history and word-use frequencies, he had become audibly aroused.

"Caleb? Caleb!"

What was this? He started from his reverie, his cerebration. He found that he was in a place of dining, but apparently not alone tonight. He had forgotten. The meal was not yet begun.

In a long, low hall, under shimmering

geometric lights and before a virgin tablecloth, he sat. The table was circular, one of many in the same chamber. Before him, all the utensils of food-taking glittered in fine array: the silver was ornate with tame flourishes. He held his space at board like a flea at the edge of an immense button. To his left, a co-worker was murmuring dyspeptically, anonymously.

"Caleb!"

It was Mona, another graphic artist from the workshop. His colleague. To his right. They were all here; almost everyone from the company was. He did not recall having ordered a meal. His lips and tongue felt somewhat used and tired, as if he had been speaking. What had he said? She was whispering insistently to him.

"...whatsoever, and I don't see how anyone could say otherwise. Anyone can see it. Particularly you. Or you should. Don't be *childish*. I'm certain this will all lead to the best possible end-state. It's efficient and it's necessary. And it's necessary because it's efficient. Nature's like that. Do you remember last time with the payroll people, the fuss? That woman made such a scene. Petty. Irrational. And blind! She just couldn't see..."

In the middle of the table a vase of flowers stood, chromatic. The static blooms yearned upward, out of a wicker vase, empty and with no space for water at the bottom – more of a sconce, Caleb thought – and scented the air with light polymer notes. The colors were immense, very saturated, while the blossoms themselves opened upward, straining at him like plastic lips, eager for kisses. Very accessible. He liked it.

"…where are they all now? Hmmm? Well, I told you it would be better this way and I was right because you just have to let them do their job, make their choices, and everything will turn out well in the end. It's all about utility. Everything maximizes utility, as long as you let it. It can look bad at the time, in the little world, but in the big world it only gets better and – hey, hey you – it always gets better and I've seen it and you've seen it, so I wish you wouldn't say such awful trash or ask such silly questions. It gives me a headache and I wanted to enjoy myself tonight. I *dressed* for this," and then she raised her hands to her temples. All her bracelets clattered, cluttered down to her elbows and she made little medicinal circles with her fingertips.

"Of course," said Caleb, turning so that he could be better seen as he gradually recalled why they were there that night, what he had just said. "Getting rid of all of them seemed simply immoderate to me, that is all. Doing it all at once? We naturally have to modernize, automate, find ways to simplify where we can. It's just…"

"What?"

He shrugged. He looked good when he did it, too, glistening with fine oils. "An insurance firm should have an actuary or two on staff, I feel.

Even if the predictions have gotten that good. Just in case."

"Why?"

"I only think that…"

"Huh!" she proclaimed and made a great show of not caring what he said next. Caleb's attention drifted to an overweight Asian seated meditatively across the table from them. He appeared to be dozing, but could have been simply lost in thought. Did he look upset at all? This man was among the staff that had been made redundant by a new algorithm and whose severance was to be commemorated tonight. Caleb recalled with uncertainty that his position had been surprisingly senior. Further, that he was known for his fondness for paper and would print documents with a will, stacking them in high, harmonious piles, indexed, on his desks and cabinets. The company had otherwise eliminated material records long ago and there was no means of processing this waste, and he had for years made use of a personal shredder to dispose of his unwanted files, surreptitiously tipping the refuse into his office's ventilation shaft and who knew where it went after that? His eyes were closed serenely and his mouth shut in a tiny upward pout, like a pensive mackerel's. Mona had diverted her attention to her compact, where she busied herself for a few moments with primping. The Asian, a Korean, remained inert.

Food then came. "I love how you don't even

have to order anymore!" Mona enthused, reengaging in conversation, and she gave her hands a crisp, little clap, fingertips to palm. "They just *know* what you want." The waiter silently settled her meal in the middle of a ring of silverware. Bright vegetables steamed on her plate, clustered close as hedgehogs, warm and inviting. She chirped in appreciation. Caleb considered his own food: a poorly-executed steak held center stage, dyes leeching out of it to pollute what appeared to be potatoes and other, less certain offerings. He inhaled deeply over it and took in the smell of some sort of chemical, fennel-like flavoring. Fork in hand, he tapped the ribeye experimentally, as if it were the surface of a tambourine. It was all synthetic, but still managed to look somehow undercooked. He duly pared his meats down to size and began to stir everything together.

"Oh, I wish you wouldn't do that."

He looked up. Mona had already subtracted two little puffs of color from her platter. The Asian, meanwhile, had bowed his head to say grace over a platter of gelatinous forms. Other diners busied themselves in their own ways.

"What?"

"That."

"This?"

"That." She indicated his plate.

"I eat like this."

"I know. There's something wrong with it. It doesn't make sense. I don't like that you do it."

"It's just food. I can do what I like with it." He continued to circulate the tines of his fork around his meal, homogenizing. Mona lunged forward and made an urgent flutter at him to get him to stop. He persisted. She made a squeak.

"I think it's obscene!" she hissed. "Obscene!" His blessing finished, the Korean – Yoon? Possibly. Maybe Moon? – righted himself and began to lovingly consume what he had been daily given. He murmured low and to himself. Mona pivoted back so that her head sat with its chin slightly inclined into her neck and eyed Caleb with disdain, while her silver glinted. "I'm not surprised they can't find anyone for you. You're vulgar."

"Oh, I need no help. In fact, I enjoyed a lovely evening with a lady I met on my own, just last night. We had quite the experience."

"No, you didn't. And everyone needs help these days." She grimaced as Caleb took nourishment. "Oh good God."

"Her name is Lisa," Caleb smacked, lying. In a trice, a quarter of his platter had been suctioned. "She works at the ice rink. I made an impression as I rented skates from her and we started talking. She is new to the building and very lonely."

"I hate it when you do this," Mona countered. "I hate your stupid little stories."

"We went to the cinema after she finished at

work and then took an intimate walk up on the roof. Such stars… I caressed her by moonlight and she is desperate to see me again." His mouth was completely full of food. "We will tryst anon, tonight, as soon as our meal here is concluded." He swallowed and tapped his fingers on the tabletop, chanting quietly "Lee-*sa*! Lee-*sa*! Lee-*sa*!" and his face did not change.

"What, and I suspect her parents are from Neptune and own a methane ranch?"

"Why, how did you know? Yes, they are from Neptune and own a methane ranch. I've seen pictures. And they –"

"That is so inappropriate! Stop it! I want you to stop! *Stop* before I…" and she was cut off. The flower arrangement in the middle of the table began suddenly to huff. Caleb and Mona both turned; from the base of the bouquet, a faint, regular breathing came forth to touch the ear. Other diners at the table took notice as well and paused to listen. It was the heavy respiration of an elderly man, high and low, irregular in pitch, but with a tempo like a metronome. For a moment it ceased and Caleb lifted his rear from the seat to look among the stalks, at their base.

"Friends!" a voice came, unexpected. "Friends, I apologize for interrupting you. I need but a moment of your time."

"Look!" hissed Mona and pointed, again. At the far end of the hall, Caleb could discern the executive, Old George, risen from his chair to speak, microphone in hand. He was but a portly blob, floating above the heads of other attendees in a different field of focus.

"The boss!"

Caleb remained silent. He lowered himself into his seat.

"Friends, I want … you all for … being here today. It is important for Longshot Insurance and also … your own lives. As it is for me, myself. And as we, we move forward, into tomorrow, into next year, it is important to remember … role you have played, and … even now, in our development." The connection was horrible and chunks of George's speech were gapping out. None of Caleb's co-workers seemed much to care, though they paused in their chewing and smacking while the voice continued.

At the table's far end, the Possible Yoon nodded, as if in appreciation.

"We move … ever forward, all of us," continued Old George, who, with this speech, was marking the severance of much of the company's remaining staff. "And we move along trajectories marked off before us which we are obliged to follow. For whatever happens … as it was to happen, and we know it … that way." More breathing followed and Yoon – yes, Caleb was certain of it now – nodded his approval again, showing signs of rising animacy. He straightened, unfolded his arms and laid his hands on his thighs, palms upward, bracketing his pelvis. His eyes were opened; he seemed attentive.

"Friends, let us remember … something must happen. Something always happens, though … not apparent at the moment." Mona dove into the plastic canopy, her fingers piloting into the foliage like the delicate, sensitive beak of an exotic water fowl, dipping into a stream to murder snails. The connection improved. "We move, we live not at random. And as one object, cast, collides with another, let us not see it as two bodies crushing into conflict, but as one rushing into the waiting embrace of a welcoming partner." He breathed again. "It is not strange. It is natural. Very natural. It is good that the river empties into the sea. It is good that the sea gives its water to the cloud, it is good, too, for the rain to fall in the meadow, and it is good for the water of the plain to gather, pool, and feed the river that will find the ocean again, though the ocean be different from what it once was, it is still good. And today is good, as well."

Yoon lowered his head, as if in receipt of sacrament. Caleb felt that if he were to speak at this moment, raise his voice, the Korean might cast something violently at him. Mona fidgeted.

"Now, don't you remember the motto for our gay little company, Longshot? It's so simple. Here." And he intoned:

High though the sky is and wide…

"Come now, finish it with me," he called and Caleb could see him raise his arms in the distance. A shuffling chorus came up as the assembled employees droned at their plates in unison:

...it's ours for today and tomorrow.

"You've all made me happy. I am so happy," Old George continued colorlessly, "today. I am very happy. Tomorrow, there is a new initiative for our corporation, a new product that Longshot will unveil. But that is not for now. You should be here now, as you are. Enjoy. Eat as you will… Dine. It is very pleasing." Breathing. "Let us think of tomorrow: it will be as today, but broader, wider. Wherever you are."

Far off, the rotund figure raised a speck in his hand. Muffled applause followed. Yoon's face showed with contentment, delight, his eyes charged with tears. And then he fell on his meal, devouring in a pious snarf the three remaining cubes that lay on his plate. He leaned back and the water streamed down the sides of his face, wetted his cheeks. He seemed so happy. Mona chattered her way through the remains of her repast, abstracting morsels from the whole until nothing remained.

Caleb looked down to face his orts. Chunks of muted color, screwed together, gazed up upon him. Expectation. He took up again the fork and laid it into the mashed pabulum, circling the plate with it in a practiced motion. He took up his bites, took in the mash, and, by degrees, the residue of his repast was diminished. With intimate care he supped upon the scraps, made them of his Self. The confused pap curled in his belly and gradually diffused. He was sated. And, though he had taken it into his digestion, nestled it in his innards, his unstained shell had remained stainless, again. He laid his fork down and listened to the sound around him for a while, as the meal drew to its natural close. He stared at Mona a little. Then he rose and left with the rest.

2

Coming to a halt outside Old George's office the next day, Caleb thought to himself. "Lee-*sa*!" he thought, standing expressionlessly. "Lee-*sa*! Methane ranch! Nep-*tune*!" and he raised a hand to touch the knot of his handsome cravat, sensing its alignment, which was perfect. It bisected his shirtfront, lying along the line that divided his mirror eyebrows, his finely finished shoes. He stared down at the toe-tips and tried to discern his face in the polished leather. Found he couldn't. "Lee-*sa*!" Everyone needs help these days? He raised his hand to the boss's door and knocked, then suffered a full-body fidget; he recovered and held himself smart and secure. He was the image of rectitude and self-restraint. There was a buzz, the lock lifted, and the door swung.

The high office of the CEO, Longshot Insurance, was of a unique design, centered around the innovative heating system. White columns of patterned ceramic stood at patient intervals in parallel rows to the right and to the left, punctuating the length of the room. They were hollow; inside were ducts that communicated with the server rooms deep in the basement. The operation of these computers warmed the air about them, which rose and was conveyed from that space, as exhaust, through channels that made a network through the building's whole height, linking at last to Old George's chambers at the apex.

Around the base of each column ran a ring of little pores, ever so small, and also around the base of the dynast's chair (mounted on a little silver belly-button that permitted him to swivel about as he engaged in his office). The vault's temperature was regulated through the modulation of these ports, which would dilate to permit air to diffuse with a sibilant *hiss* into the office, while the rest was expelled through vents on the roof. The pillars were load-bearing and sustained the weight of the ceiling above, so the walls were given over entirely to clear glass, ribboned with faint seams, and the sun gave a glorious, purifying light, all very pleasing to someone.

Otherwise, the room was sparse and contained little; Caleb could not make himself enter without first washing his hands. The ablutions… The columns were hydrophobic and always gleamed – bright, white, and antiseptic – cool to the touch.

Caleb walked the length of the space and paused to stand before the table while the old man played solitaire; there were many cards already on the table in front of him. It was something he did often, and Caleb had witnessed the practice before. With technique, George drew, considered, placed, discarded, drew, considered, placed, discarded, drew, considered… and the little cavalcades on the desktop lengthened until he had found a way to arrange the entire deck. The thing done, he would lean back and draw his mouth across his face into a tight line, like a smile, as he considered the order he had made. Then he would slurry the cards together into a chaos again, assemble a little pile on the broad, executive mahogany, and begin the exercise afresh. He could do it for hours and he was doing it now. Caleb stood and waited for the boss to bring his attention forward. There was a strange smell in the room, almost mineral, and he found it disconcerting. The center of his gravity started to drift in a lazy, languid loop while he waited, and his eyes unfocused, slightly. He huffed in a deep breath of it, whatever it was. The atmosphere, its vapors, made him feel dreamsy-weamsy and yet very wide awake.

George inhaled deeply, flexed his hands. Laid his hands in his lap, tongued at his teeth, stretched his neck. Adjusted his glasses. He laid his hands now on the table, balled them into fists, and laid them on the table again, flat. Caleb wondered if he intended to discuss the new initiative, revealed last night.

"We had a payout, Caleb," Old George announced.

"A payout?"

"Mm-hmm. A payout."

"A big one?"

"Mm-hmm."

"What do we do?"

"Mm-hmm. A payout. Big one. Cashing in."

The last time a policy-holder had actually been able to collect on their plan had been years ago. Caleb's bowels contorted and the juices of his recent meal squelched. His hackles raised. Trying to attract little attention to the motion, he raised a hand to his abdomen and gave his tum-tum a stealthy pat. Under his breath, he belched.

"Sir, what do we do?"

George had been staring at the cards before him as if trying to tell a fortune. He looked up now and gave Caleb the full moon of his face, round as a clock and no hands at all.

"I'm not entirely certain, to be honest."

"What did we do last time?"

"I don't remember. That was years ago."

"Years?" Caleb played dumb, politely.

"Six years? I think. The one at the airport."

"The heiress?" Caleb offered. The heiress had been demented. An elderly lady, very much attached to animals, she was gibbering on the tarmac waiting to board a domestic flight when her pet carrier had come open and the occupant, a young goat, had capered out. She'd pursued it to her misfortune as first the kid and then she herself had been sucked into the red-hot intake port of the craft, carbonized, and pulsed out the rear as dehydrated exhaust. She had been *very* deceased. Her death was unfortunate and the damage to the plane was horrific, but Longshot had been liable for neither of them. Unfortunately and however, half of her organs had been metallic transplants used in a course of scientific study and insured by the parent company, which sought damages. Once her blackened residue had been suctioned from the apron and proven to be of zero research value, payment was made; it had been painful to the insurer. After a thorough review, the company's risk-assessing mechanisms had been updated and there had been no further claims. Caleb doubted her half-remembered experience would serve as much of a guide here, if it had been repeated. "Yes, her," he confirmed. "The heiress."

Old George seemed to receive this information but did not offer a response. His attention was engaged with something in the distance. There was a pause. Caleb waited, holding himself tight. The pause lengthened.

"You've been producing recently?" George questioned, in a tone that did not perceive any change in topic. He had lifted his head so that their eyes met.

"Of course, sir," Caleb responded. "Haven't missed in months and averaging twelve-point-four finished pieces a week with an impact ratio of seven-to-two." *Exact!* "Market variance is scheduled to be about 3.2% again this quarter, and I've been able to regularly hit about five-out-of-seven suggested elements, now that we've improved the queries."

"Excellent numbers, Caleb."

"Thank you, sir," he said with a little preen and a puff, haunches clenched tight. "I know their importance in evaluating my portfolio." And he did.

"Caleb, I…"

"Yes?"

"Hold on. Let me show you this. I…"

"Sir?"

George was fumbling with something below the surface of the table. "I can't find it."

"Sir, if you were to let me…"

"No."

"Sir, but I could just…"

"Stop. Wait. Here it is."

And he lifted up into Caleb's view a still image, on glossy stock and cut to standard size. It was grubby and horribly, horribly rumpled, almost mauled. He held it gingerly with a cocked, grimacing pinky.

"You didn't do this one, did you?" he asked, levelly, extending it towards Caleb, across the wood. "Records show you did." The surface finish was peeling off at the corners and the undertones were visible peeping through, incomplete.

"Sir!" he affirmed. He had. It was a piece from one of their homeowners' packages, a bundle of policies offered together at a calculated rate. The name of the package stood dominant at the top, dressed in comely serifs and arrayed in balanced proportion to the company logo at the bottom. Policy information followed: fire, lightning strike, earthquake, etc., framed in compartments placed here, here, and here. There were bullets that gave particulars. Fine print. Good. All good. In the middle of all the disaster words and figures stood a representation of a quaint, cadmium yellow house, the thing protected. He remembered designing it. It was done in simple lines, an unimpressive structure with white trim. Squinting a little, he saw that there were soft grasses bowing in the warm wind; he could feel the wetness of the dew tingling in his palms, and when the flowers opened it was very special. The structure and its grounds were ornamented with fruit – little fruits that shone in the spring rain as if enameled – elm, and vines, and the place had a particular fragrance. Out of sight, beyond the hill, there was a small lake where silver fish shimmered, under the sun.

"Caleb, take your hands off my table."

Caleb took his hands off his table.

"Is this your work? Did you do this?"

"Yes, sir. I did. Of course I did. Natural disasters were high that week, I remember. So was danger to the home. I could have gotten more 'nest' imagery in there if I'd wrapped the house in ivy, which I probably should have. But it's mine, either way."

"Then she's yours, too."

"Who?"

"The lady, the payout. Caleb, you need to do something about this woman," George said. "This is the piece she responded to when she came in and you're the one who generated it. So it follows, Caleb, that you're the one who will find a way to fix her. We don't have accountants anymore, not since the payroll system went in. We have no lawyers, not since we automated compliance. There is no staff to handle the situation and I know we don't have the institutional memory needed to make this happen on our own anymore. I don't know how to do it. This wasn't supposed to happen, Caleb. I don't see how it could have, not since the changes we made after your heiress." *His* heiress? Had Caleb somehow owned her? Procured her? "But it's obvious that all this goes back to you. Therefore, you're the one who will find us a way out." He made no real attempt to persuade, nor was he overtly aggressive. He seemed to think instead that, one thing implying another, Caleb would just pick up on what he needed to do. It was warm in the room and his skin showed with a light, dry sweat. "You will do this. You *will* find a way to deal with this situation, this customer. And if this somehow becomes a serious issue, it may imperil the future of Longshot's next project." He was very compelling. "Our reputation must remain unassailable, you understand? Intact."

"Who is it?" Caleb pushed, staying on target. He was very professional. "The claimant, what's her name?"

"Vera."

Vera?

"I've taken her on as a janitor; we can still hire those. But her claim is large and she'll need to be on payroll, for six hundred and twenty-eight years before it's paid in full. That doesn't work. I'll have information on the situation and the client forwarded to your account."

"And you want me to find a way to take care of her?"

"You will find a way to take care of her." Caleb considered. He thought he saw an opportunity to get something he wanted. What was that thing? He wasn't certain, didn't know, but saw the opening to pursue it anyway. He wanted to speak, gently at first, about his needs. He would layer one sentence upon another, mortaring them together with his pathos. Lathering up his emotions, he would let the words slide out, let everything flow. "Direct access!" he would say. "Meaningful contact!" His tone would rise; he would continue to speak. His rhythm and tone could then heighten and his throat and lips work. He might importune. Leaning forward, he would reach in, looking for a link, a bridge into the "yes". His desire, ill-formed and resistant to crisp articulation, rose in him to a vague, commanding presence. He sensed himself wandering, not on the same line as George and not able to get on it. "This is vital!" he wanted to insist, qualifying whatever would have just come before. It would be nice if George agreed, wouldn't it? Maybe he might. He was impressed with himself.

"Caleb."

Caleb?

"Take your hands off my table."

Caleb removed his hands again. If he had been less fastidious about himself, his grooming, he might have left prints.

"Look. Caleb. You. Will do. This. And. This. Is how. It will. Be." Tick. Tock. His face was a clock. Tickery. Tockery. Caleb felt denial and pressure to comply. He nodded and smoothed over a portion of his cuff, eliminating wrinkles.

"Good. Get to it then. I have a teleconference about the new 'Microinsurance' effort in five." And then the meeting was over: George made a small sign, touched himself, and that concluded everything. Caleb took his leave and walked a straight line, back to the door that had admitted him. It closed now, after his passage, pressing carefully shut and him secure without. For a moment he stood with his gaze directed down the corridor. The lines to his left, right, top, and bottom all cambered forward to a point, training him onward. Doors peeped at shrinking intervals, waiting to enlarge at his approach. One gaped beside him and he turned to read the plaque beside the door beside his person:

C. Ezekiel Yoon

And below that:

Senior Executive Actuary

Looking in, Caleb could see that it was all bare; nothing personal remained. Pieces of office furniture roamed, cropping at the gray carpet about a box of administrative supplies, and a portrait of the radiant Founder stared out from the wall, seeing nothing of the little there was to see. Caleb's eyes flicked about the room, appraising, cataloging its contents, and then he checked an urge to rummage. Instead, he pirouetted back to the hallway and permitted himself to be funneled down it.

He walked down the hall, turned a corner. Walked. Walkery. Tickery. Tockery. Talkery. The white, white walls surrounded, arounded him and the floor near the ceiling of the near-empty building as he walked with the tread of a man so soon dead and his feet were like lead as he one two one two one. He realized he was raising his knees a little high in his gait, pointing his hoofs a little. No one had seen him. He was on his way to do something that made sense, George's bidding, as he bid. It was a sober task and he would do it. Sober, yes, oh so very sober. He adjusted himself, over-corrected, toe-to-heel, heel-to-toe, toe and heel slowly forward… Except for George's office, the entire upper floor was empty; any mosquito trapped up there was doomed to slow starvation. Buzzzzzz… he was ringing for the elevator. It came and he rode it down, straight down, floors and floors down, down to the level where he worked. He walked out, into another passageway, then to his studio.

Inside the workspace, everything was dressed in cool shades. Five design stations were spaced equidistantly, around an empty center: his, those of three absent coworkers, the manager's (elevated), and Mona's. She was present, attired in frosted gray silk, upright, and intently drawing circles. Her right elbow chicken-winged up and down in repetitive industry.

She heard his heel click on the threshold. With a push, she turned. "You!" she cried. "Oh, thank goodness it's you!"

Caleb stopped short; the response was not typical. Mentally, he pursed his lips and narrowed his eyes, gathering inner order.

"I thought *she* might have come back!" Mona grimaced horribly, baring most of her upper gum area in an attitude that implied, simultaneously, nausea and fear, as if she'd been visited by a banshee, bearing dead fish. "She touched *everything*! She put her *hands* on everything!" Her little nostrils pulsed.

"Excuse me?" He was guarded. "I do not know what you are talking about."

"Look!" she commanded. "See?" she inquired, and straightened an arm and finger to indicate his carrel. About her wrist a fine, golden bangle, much larger in diameter than her forearm, rocked as she pointed.

He looked. His workspace was plain: just a lamp, a stand, and the design surface. He saw now that it was horribly smeared, as if a riot of school children gone off their medication had all seen puppies on the inside and crowded over at once, in a rush of noses, lips, and puffy, huffy breath. It was unsanitary. He drew a disinfectant wipe and briskly sterilized the whole thing. His own reflection emerged, looking back at him from an angle, below. He powered up the screen and it was lost in a block of light.

"Vera!"

"Vera?"

"Yes! She came by, half an hour ago. Said she was the new janitor, come to the see the place. Then she, she…" Mona's words, drawn out, failed, then returned to her as rush of physical energy. She drew her hands in almost-fists up to the spaces near her cheeks and her face paled. In the air about her, her polished fingernails floated like a manicured constellation, Agittarius. Breathing became difficult and she expelled righteous bursts of hateful air through her teeth and nose. The motion overflowed and involved her shoulders. "She touched *everything*!"

"Mona. It can't have been that bad."

"She said she was going to the third floor. Do you even *know* what's down there? Want to see what she's up to? I bet we can find her. I have access to the cameras. Let's see what's going on!" She turned face-to-face with her interface and smiled in the spin. The chicken wing reappeared.

"What's on the third floor?"

"Nothing. Does it matter? Where is she?"

"I thought accounting used to be down there or something. It's an awfully long ways down from here."

"Accounting? Probably. Or something like it."

"Look!" and she recoiled from the display, pointing like a proud Retriever. A figure had appeared onscreen.

"That's her?"

"Yep. The hair. I'm certain. Perfect match."

He looked. The third story had not seen maintenance in a long time, as it had been one of the first to be emptied. But it had been opulent once, sporting a balcony that let out into the atrium, which was open to the two floors below. He remembered small string ensembles playing there at company functions under a mist of promise, during events years ago. That area, partially visible from the street, was probably still given an auto-brush every now and again, but

Caleb was looking into a different room entirely: the reception hall. It, too, had once been grand. Through the dusty aperture he could see the parquet: rich, Semitic curls of woods, delicately mated. There was no furniture. A single female figure stood near the middle of the room, a little off-center, her back facing the lens. Mona put the focus on her.

She was a stocky woman: pale, big, and round of body. Heavy, in an energetic way. Her shoulders curved in powerful, downward slopes. Dressed in some sort of custodial uniform, the canvas stretched taut across the upper back with wide legs that hung loose around her sneakers. Mona had been honest about the hair; from underneath a tight-fitting cap, it issued in a pale, buoyant cloud. She was vigorously manipulating a mop in a bucket of cleanser and as she went up-down-up-down-up-down with the rhythm of the work, the mane bouncing behind her, half a step off. This agitation was so violent that she had worked a good deal of solution free of the container, and she now stood in an irregular pool of it, which spread in all directions. With a jerk she pulled the mop-head clear of the bucket and then held it in suspense, dripping just inches above the ground, before carefully lowering it onto the woodwork. She began pushing it about with meditated care, feet planted, in gradually widening circles.

"Can we get audio? Can we hear her?"

"Sure! No mysteries *here…*" Mona punched and jabbed. "Can you hear that? How about now?" And there was sound. They could hear Vera crooning.

She was making a modulating sort of moaning noise that pitched higher and lower with the motion of her staff. The radius of the work soon widened so that she was mopping about herself, making dynamic, purposeful spins on silent feet. Then she stops, draws herself upright, and holds the thing close to her. The sensitivity of the microphone is such that the murmur of language registers, but neither of them can make out what is said. There are muscles working there, under the tunic.

"Yes, oh yes," she coos, her voice rising just enough to be intelligible. She has an accent? "Splooshy-sploosh with the kindly-whoo and who's the dancing dandy? With the drums? Hmmm…? Has somebody hurt you, O my dear?" She draws the rod closer, letting it pucker into the fabric of her garb. "Hmmm…?" She extends an arm to hold her partner at an angle, then cups her other beneath it in support. They move together, inscribing a small clover in the dust beneath them. The tempo quickens as they widen their arc again, Vera's hands gripping, moving, sliding, everywhere.

"Hah!" she calls out. "Hah!" Mona grimaces and raises her hands halfway to stop her ears.

They are prancing very quickly now, the two

of them, the intent of cleaning the room – if ever it existed – completely forgotten. Vera spins and drops down low, very low, supporting her companion only a few inches from the ground. Her footwork shows mindless dexterity, her soles pulse up and down in a rapturous rapping. In the pooled cleanser, her feet squeak and flash, faster yet and faster still, until finally…

"No!" she calls out, separating. She falls!

The mop flies free, free from her grasp. Sailing beyond the camera's frame, Caleb hears it concuss and clatter artless on the ground. "Oh, no! No! Nonononononono!" Vera's body sagged, heavier than a moment ago as she surged to hurry over, her broad white face wrought with woe. She ran, ducking briefly off-screen, and then returned with the mop cradled senseless in her arms.

Caleb followed her, his eyes fixed. She trailed her own ponderous feet back to the bucket and stared down into the dirty water. With gravity, she held the lifeless object forward with one heavy arm, parallel to the surface of the earth. The thick, tangled strands of the mop-head hung just above the fluid, touched it, and were then submerged as she lowered it in. She then crouched over the pail and seemed to work it with her hands, but her form interposed between the camera and the action, so Caleb could not see what she was doing.

She held the squat for a while and all that could be heard was the play of liquids in motion. Then she raised her voice and they heard her speaking, dolefully:

> We strut beneath the wave and dance on sand
> Earth rising where we stand;
> Fish titter as we race,
> And coral part apace
> Shrinking at His command,
> As on we go. The marlin gapes
> In worship as he sees our forms, our shapes
> Incise, cut through the waving drapes
> Of seaweed on the ocean floor.
> Above, the basking seals roar;
> The otters keen, upon the shore.
> "Your goading wounds the sea will tend
> "O, Grace to Man,
> "O, Grace to Man,
> "Your bones will knit, Your flesh will mend."

"Oh goodness, this is terrible," said Mona. "Oh this is bad. You don't do that with a mop, that's not what it's *for*. And if you'd seen her when she as up here... Do you see what I mean now that you've –" but she was interrupted. The audio link was still open and Vera repeated again the final four lines,

> *"Your goading wounds the sea will tend*
> *"O, Grace to Man,*
> *"O, Grace to Man,*
> *"Your bones will knit, Your flesh will mend."*

This was Vera.

3

"Washington? Washington can you hear us?" It was a teleconference. The Pacific Northwest office could not be reached.

Caleb sat at a round table with twenty of his co-workers staring at the uncooperative screen as the officiant fiddled with the controls. Two weeks had passed. A small pile of his materials lay in a neat pyramid before him. Tablet, stylus, and things.

"Washington? Hello!" The man with the remote raised his voice and gestured, as if this would somehow improve his chances of being heard in a state capital on the opposite coast. "Gah!" he exasperated and stabbed at the panel. "Washington!"

The image onscreen suddenly resolved. "Hello?" a cheery face emerged.

"Oh thank goodness," Caleb's office rep breathed in relief. "Are we coming in clear?"

"We are fine!" affirmed the voice of the worker from afar. "Hello!"

"Right. Quiet, everyone! Quiet!" the chief celebrant commanded. "Silence! We have much to do!" and he raised his hands. The room was hushed in obeisance.

From this point forward, Caleb knew pretty well what to do. Each participant rose and spoke in turn, lifted their separate voices in accordance with protocol and Rules of Order, one-by-one-by-one. Everyone was very excited about the initiative. Microinsurance! The announcement had been made only yesterday. But what an idea! No one really knew what it was… nevertheless, as a fresh campaign, a new line of products and policies from Longshot, it promised opportunity. Figures scrolled on the display, indicating – not telling or obscuring, but indicating – the most appropriate course of action, and Old George had even presented a vision statement:

> We will deliver, come storm and wind;
>> Raindrops, numbered and counted.

No one had a clue what it meant, though there had been no objections. Caleb's turn to contribute came and went. It gave him a sense of catharsis to speak, to be seen in this company; when he re-seated himself, he was cleansed. Feeling fresher than he'd been before, he watched in appreciation as the few who came after him rose to fill their roles until, finally, everything had been said, and everyone had had their chance to say it. At the end, the man conducting the meeting made brief mention, as a personnel note, that Caleb's direct manager had gotten his hand caught in a garbage disposal and ground it down to a stub. He would not be returning to the office. Everyone was relieved that the meeting was close to over.

There was a clear tone and the connection ended. Their host made a gesture, bidding them to rise and all rose; none seemed to have pressing business and there was evident a general reticence to leave. On the side table where refreshments were usually set out, a few gnarled, drought-stricken house plants displayed themselves and the congregation instinctively started migrating in that direction. Chatter warmed the room, rising with a uniform, natural heat. The attendees spaced themselves in Doric order, directed at each other, speaking. Caleb faced Sophie, the hyperactive technician from down the hall and cousin to one of his officemates. Her face was kind of squashed; the countenance was very narrow, but her genes had spaced the eyes so widely so that Caleb felt that she trapped him in the field of her vision, rather than centered him in it. Her teeth projected and her mouth was not naturally closed at rest, so her dry tongue was usually visible. She was professionally engaged arranging clip art of savage, almost-certainly extinct beasts in enticing patterns to sell animal attack policies, coupled with safari cruise tickets sold by another company. Her breasts were gigantic. Caleb had made ardent protestations of sincerest affection, but met only with arid denial. "I've checked," she would breathe. "It won't work." He'd rooted vigorously about her edges a couple times more, like a pig that is sure of a phantom truffle, but ultimately given up. Privately, he questioned her sexuality.

"I've heard you're dealing with the claimant," she said at him.

"I am," he confirmed.

"And that you were talking to people high up about this?"

"I was," he confirmed.

"Well, I hope that you deal with it soon, then."

"I will," he confirmed, focusing on her tear ducts.

And his efforts to resolve the Vera issue had, later that day, led him to an obscure section of the building. In Caleb's mind, the problem seemed easily enough solved. Longshot had never been an altruistic venture, an organization that held the anxieties, longings, and spiritual broodings of the human soul to be of any concern. Instead, its temple had always been the world, from whose vitality and movement it sought to nourish itself to the exclusion of all others, like the fat, gurgling twin of a one-tit mother. And the cretin merchants who had bored the first holes in the rock here, lain the earliest foundations, had been determined to thrive on a continuous holocaust of fatted cattle, even if they deserved none of it at all. It followed that getting any money out of the company as a claimant, even when duly and legally owed, was a process as delicate and convoluted as a butterfly intestine, and that opportunities for wreckage abounded. Caleb sought to exploit one such fragility in the supplicant's claim and had realized that a nice, heavy chain was all he needed to make this happen. So he got one. He carried the clinking links with him now, with a lock and a key and a bounce in his stride.

"Claimant," dry policy intoned, "shall forfeit all rights to compensation for any policy of any sort if Claimant shall depart the premises of Longshot Insurance without having completed all appropriate pre-processing procedures to advance his or her claim for remuneration." In Caleb's cunning estimation, Old George had erred terribly in choosing to take Vera on as he did, for in doing so he had granted to her all the rights and privileges of a company employee (to include access to all on-site facilities) and she had, for a whole week, not left the building. She showered in the gym, took her meals in the cafeteria, and slept on the dormitory level, all while continuing her enthusiastic, irregular mopping. She had also received an account on the company communication system, and had since kept herself busy harassing everyone in the company directory with nonsensical, multicolored messages. Furthermore, she had so far shown no interest in making her way to the office where the paperwork required to draw on her deserved funds awaited, but there was no telling when she might. Of course, it was questionable whether she would be able to do anything even if she made it to the Claims Office – which was marked on no maps, pointed to in no direction signs, and hidden in a corner of the edifice, deep in a snarl of hallways – as there was no longer any staff employed to process her application and the procedures involved were bizarre, arcane, and opaque. But Caleb and his swinging fetters had decided to head out there and solve the problem for good. If, he reasoned, he was able to secure the place permanently against her ingress, it was only a matter of time before Vera left of her own volition for one reason or another, and the problem sorted itself out.

On account of this stratagem, Caleb thought very highly of himself. The swing of the chain felt powerful, made *him* feel powerful too as his muscles coiled and opened under the weight of the thing. He had twisted the heavy rings in his broad palms and mused upon his certain, future laurels. His confidence in his own success on this point was so strong that he had not even bothered to look into Vera's file yet. What point would there have been? Indeed! What would be the point?

Oh, how snubbed he felt when he came to that door and found it had no handle! Nor hook! Nor any other place to fix his chain! The thing was mounted to swing inward and its only external feature was a flat plate at shoulder height where one was supposed to push. He faced the uncooperative portal, fists bunched up high on his hips, the chain dangling weakly to his knees...

His brains chugged. He pivoted to look down the hallway, seeking for an object that might serve as a mooring. It was empty: there were no fixtures, was no furniture; it was silent: there was no chatter, were no footsteps. Frustrating. Turning back to face forward, he looked at the door again. In his mind he imagined the sudden sprouting of a little knob, perfect for his need and exact to his expectations. Nothing happened. He snorted and pawed at the ground a little. Perhaps there was something inside the room? Perhaps? Yes! Within, a solution! He would probe! Probe, internally, and find what lay within. Yes, yes, yes. There was a small sensor to the right of the frame; he pressed his thumb against it, requesting access. Little lights flashed for him in a circle, round and round. Granted! He laid his hand to the panel and pushed and pushed again.

The door swung, slowing as a yielding obstruction impeded, near the farthest extent of its arc. As he entered the unlit room, dust rose within and combed at his nostrils with tapered fingers.

"Mwahh-yuh!"

He staggered, reeling from the ambush on his sensitive membranes.

"Mwwhh-wuhh-wuhh…"

His hand rose to his nose, ascending through the miasma to cup his face. Up on his toes he went, back arched, heels free, chin lifted, eyes up, and mouth, the mouth, his mouth way open.

"Mwhpfsh!" Caleb said.

He clipped forward, curling inward like a shrimp, with a percussive shot. At this stimulation the room illumined, flushing with color. "Wuffuhahmuff." The chamber was very irregular, most irregular. Though his eyes watered, Caleb saw in the sudden light that a great drift of whiteness projected from the far wall and invaded upon the chamber's middle space, a huge, snowy mound, higher than he was tall.

Standing just inside the threshold, Caleb's wingtips toed its circumference. Beside it, the surfaces of furniture and fixtures were layered with dust. What automated scrubber or janitor had passed recently by this space, in execution of their duties? None, obviously. It had been long since he'd been in the personal presence of uncleanliness of almost any type, really. And shabby as the rest of the room was, the mound of whiteness in its middle seemed groomed somehow, as if recently refreshed. He glanced upward, above the level of his head, and saw the apex of it issued from a ventilation port, a wide grate up there in the wall, hard by the ceiling. He put his person in motion to duck a little and push a hand forward into it, near the base. It was paper, all paper, carried down from the ducts above, connecting to an office higher up. He withdrew his hands and turned his palms up. Superfine flakes of white and print showered down. He stood again. The upper portion of one document had made it through whole, and he lifted it out of the powder. It was pretty fresh: a time-stamp in the upper corner showed that it was printed not more than two months ago. Text filled much of its length, until it was interrupted by a slanted, frilly cut-off where some shredder had ceased its work. It ran:

Payday Loans by the Numbers

"Whence should I have flesh to give unto all this people? for they weep unto me, saying, Give us flesh, that we may eat. I am not able to bear all this people alone, because it is too heavy for me." Num. 11:13-14

The fleshpots await! With a range of comprehensive services and reasonable rates, Payday Loans by the Numbers can
relieve the suffering of your people, with established expertise, var
options

At the top, a distended cherub held a T-bone steak in the attitude of a harp, its limbs arranged in repose. Cornucopiae spewed wealth and plenty that dripped down at right angles to form corners around the announcement. Caleb appreciated the composition with the discernment of a fellow craftsman, permitting the likeness of a "fleshpot" to emerge in his mind's eye. He was uncertain what this was, but assumed it was a jug of edible tissues, which sounded nice. He let the paper fall and looked about the room again.

There was a traditional loop-handle on the inside of the door, probably ornamental, but *just* right for his purpose. But to what to attach the other end? He measured outward from this waist-high anchor at a radius of the chain's full length, spacing his feet to reach for a couple hopeless prospects. Nothing in the room would do. He looked down into the clear, bleached waste and chugged his jaw up and down a bit, thinking.

Then he turned one hand over the opposite shoulder in a readying motion, readier now, readier, until he really was ready and let the concentrated energy go. In a fell swoop he fell upon it, the knife edge of his down-turned palm leading. A spray he cast in the riven cream up about him, lifting a jet of it to his right. He advanced and another one issued to his left. Reciprocally, he scythed forward, making small, powerful steps, dynamically mincing as the fairy foam flew in flashing flights. He moved, deep to his waist, until his fingers pressed against a perpendicular hardness. In total, his advance had been a little less than three meters and the cloven slopes of his effort closed around him, like a funnel. He looked about and bored his way into the whiteness with his hands until he hit something solid again, then he peered forward. A little dark space appeared.

He bent at his knees and looked down, crannied in the little "V" he'd dug into the mix. His aperture widened and he found that he'd found a window. It was dark outside, nighttime, and he found his own face blinking back at him in reflection. With one expansive sweep, he cast his arm in a grand arc that opened up a vista of the world outside. This was a corner office? He did not know where he was in the building, other than the floor number, which was incorrectly marked in the elevators. He took a step back and lowered himself onto his haunches to regard the prospect without. Lights were on in the street. Outside, a storm was surging.

Rain heaved. Through the protective glass, he saw riotous chevrons of the downpour pulse forward, advancing. Water crushed in the streets, scrabbling at the thoroughfares, as if to tear their markings from the surface, and finding no purchase on the slickness of the walk, but still trying, laboring for that grip. It punished the tarmac. About the boulevards he saw objects cast, out of the way, as if to clear Cloud's vision of the Earth, to disencumber it. The weather laid siege to the city; the crushing wetness molested the flat surfaces and structures of the urban space beyond. And in the room it was silent; behind the vacuum-paned, clear-composite Vitrite, Caleb heard nothing, other than the ring of pressure in his ears. His hand on the glass was warm, kept warm from the storm by the gasless emptiness between the double-ply treatment and the sound of the water, the chill of the water was not absorbed but denied. His eyes didn't know where to focus and drifted forward and backward, here and there, until they found his hands on the pane. There are fine hairs on the back of his palms, and a brass bull-ring holds one finger.

And he felt the weight of his knee against something, an object. He shifted back until his heels aligned and he could survey what it was. The lip of a thing emerged, and his fingers inquired around it. Was it a table?

It was a table. With a skootch he drew it forward, out of the foam. The weight around it caved into the right and clove shut. With a couple more jerks he had it free. It was clean aluminum and positively covered with hooks, handles and purchases of all sorts. Perfect, yes perfect, as a tool of his intent. "Perfect, yes, perfect," he repeated.

He hustled it out into the open, turned it lengthwise and with a push it went out the door and into the hallway, where he rotated it so that its breadth obstructed the entrance. With a skip he was back in the room, and the chain was jingling cheerfully in his hand as he slotted it through the handle and passed it, both ends, out into the hall again, closing the door on the middle of its length. Then he zipped under the table, laced through a convenient handle with a turbulent clatter and pulled both ends tight so they met. The table scudded into the door and he snicked the lock shut through two tense little loops. A tight ribbon of openness gapped into the Claimants' Office, where the light, sensing no one's presence, turned itself off. Caleb popped out from under the table with two agile bursts and stood up to give the whole thing a looksee. He shook the assembly vigorously; it held tight. The door was effectively sealed. He passed a hand over his brow and the cloth of his dress fell into straight lines again.

It was good. Job was done. He reached into his pocket for his device to make a call to the boss and notify him of developments. When it came out, he found that he had received a message on the company-internal system. His eyes met with:

His heart pounds in the dark
    And footsteps through his veins.
    The fiber of his tendons strains:
He plants His limbs, He takes His mark
               And on the sky He trains
His eyes. I *hear* him rise.
His pulses drumming up the skies –
The sea sounds back. The salt replies.

And with his surging all the creatures dance:
The rays join hands, seahorses prance,
    The shark, the herring, and the hake
Combine to decorate his wake
 In chorus, through the thinning sea
 A great procession sun-ward swings, and in its van is He
 Alone. The tattoo of his chambered heart
Leads fin to gill in one ecstatic Art.
It's shallow now. He breaches from the school! They part.

        Old Ocean rides
        Upon all sides
        Of that small reach
        Upon the beach
    Where He stands in the tides.

He noticed immediately that the lines were not all the same length and disapproved. The colors bothered him too, for the same reason, and struck him as inappropriate. It was not company style to write in green and red and blue and orange! But he read it through a second time, just to see if there was anything important in there, scrutinizing each word in isolation. By the time he made it halfway through, he was hearing Vera's voice in the words, her warm, accented speech, slurred and soft as watercolor. She murmured at the bottom of the inhospitable depths and watched Him leave her, in His ascent. His ears detected a tapping, very regular, like water on stone in an underground place. He finished rereading the piece and looked up, then around, hunting for the source of the sound. His own foot!

On the tile! *Oh!* Oh how *dare* it! He governed his limb, putting it back in place.

He stood embarrassed. Again, no one had seen him. And he was grateful. He opened a link to George's office to complete his call. A sound purred in his ear. He had to wait for a while before George picked up.

"Yes? Hello? I was just… Hello?" Lips smacked drily.

"Hello, boss," said Caleb. "It's me." And he told him. Not in any great detail, but he laid out his thinking, his actions, and then the consequences, one-two-three.

"Sounds good," George pronounced. "Things can move forward then, sooner or later. Sounds good."

And Old George then discoursed himself, but at greater length. He talked about the future, the way ahead as it were. His vision. Now that Caleb had taken care of this troubling little matter – this matter, which would soon resolve itself, he was certain – there was a shining path to tread, away, that lead to greatness! But it needed to be done *just so*. Could he make Caleb understand? George's breath curled in his ear, assured him of the centrality of his office's work in the successful execution of this initiative. He even gave a little hint of the nature of the project. Microinsurance! Didn't the little things matter? Too often we worry about fire, earthquake, acts of God, life, death, and yet… these little things, the small parts of life, do they not deserve security? From day to day, from hour to hour, what mattered was: the enjoyment of a meal. A trip to the grandparents'. The pleasure of the next season's show. If these small parts of life were what made up life, didn't it follow that they deserved the same care as those gross, tragic events that could so easily end it?

Caleb nodded. It followed most naturally, though he grasped Old George's meaning only vaguely. There was something inspired in the geriatric voice, almost enthusiastic. He spoke like a prune that had seen an angel. "Microinsurance! Confidence, in the details!" he pressed. "Where the Devil lies!" It was totally new and it would make a splash. The people needed it, more than they knew. And it would be their, Longshot's, unique edge on the competition. It would put them at the top of the mountain, the peak of the rugged crag in the roiling sea of the industry. But it was so precious, so important, and he had to make Caleb understand.

…And did Caleb understand?

"Yes, sir. Of course."

"Good." George seemed at ease and slightly youthful, having made his meaning known. "Well, then. Get back to your desk. We all must work, play our role. We work together."

Caleb started to say something but found the line preemptively dead. Taking his hand from his ear, he saw Vera's colors once more. Then he put all of it back in his pocket and returned to his office, feeling less recognized for his efforts than would have pleased him.

In his workshop he found Mona standing by her tabletop as a tech tweaked at her station. She was bent over at the waist to bring her head level with his as he sat, and the train of her floor-length skirt hung behind her. It was patterned with soft plates, woven together, that shimmered in flickering ripples under the lamps.

4

Trend analysis had had powerful, profound implications for Caleb's work. The multiplication of Longshot's recording and analytic assets in cities meant that the pictures, the buzzwords current among the population could be isolated at any moment to be tested for impact and longevity. Those that had staying power beyond a day or two and commercial potential found their way into the produce of Caleb's office, where they were reborn as little promotional packages, packages that were blasted into the very Currents of Society, which discharged money in return. A terminal sat beside Caleb's workspace with the five most popular images of the week displayed. They were:

1. a giant cheeseburger
2. Israel (outline thereof)
3. a football helmet
4. The Resurrection
5. an atom

He grunted. There was a separate ticker for

language where keywords scrolled by at the bottom, many of them misspelled. Caleb had little direct contact with new people and all of his relationships had settled to be either essentially frustrated or functional; he used the rise and fall of the various tags as a fuzzy kind of data that he filtered through the aperture of his reason to achieve a sense of what the world was like. In his mind, he envisioned Society as a violent rope of sweaty dough with no sense of smell that obsessed morbidly over its future and could not be made to consider its past. It also stank horribly. Caleb had been at this job for four years, the recent debilitation of his leadership having now raised him to a low level in the management, and in that time had found no call to doubt any facet of this concept. Rather, he had begun to refine the likeness of this beast in his mind, which he found to live in total isolation from its own kind and yet was, by nature, cannibalistic.

Job security came to Caleb and his office through the fact that, although software had become adept at isolating those images that Society found closest to universally appealing, it could not arrange them in any manner other than serially without giving cause for confusion, disgust, or contempt. Efforts had been made, but there were not yet systems that could take representations of things as varied as Mickey Mouse, the United Nations, and a thong, and produce anything that sold insurance. Even Caleb struggled with combinations like that, but was grateful that the distributed intellect of the world produced such garbled muck that he got to remain employed.

"This Easter, don't forget to nuke your Israel Burgers^{TM} at halftime," he muttered, looking at the symbols. Somehow, he salivated. He could make a frustrated kind of sense out of most things. Did football last all year-round? He was uncertain. Probably. The words "tax atorney" limped by at the bottom. Then "suicide".

He'd found that, in extreme cases, most of the ad-space could be safely cluttered with shapes and text so that the images were divided from each other. That had nearly happened here, but the team had come through and pulled it together the day before, in a glorious effort. Still, it was bound to get some sort of reaction and the fact that this was the virgin work for George's big new project didn't really make a difference. Caleb had sold fire insurance with kittens and dental policies with pirates before. Thus, he was somewhat puzzled at George's insistence on special attention to this effort, as the policies on offer seemed to him to be a fungible mash without unique identities, and the publicity for them embodied that fact. It had to. To him, there was no doubt that this would work, as long as he made it palatable to Society.

Society! Women were either in league with Society or part of it; he was unsure of the nature of their relationship, but *convinced* of its existence. They colluded. He knew it! They formed some sort of league against him, frustrating the innocent enjoyment of his fragile blossom. In his mind he saw himself as a tender thing, undespoiled, an olive tree dandling its glistening, pendulous fruit over a stony expanse, while the females grazed on detritus and greasy scraps. How he pitied them, at times. And yet that white hot rage! They calculated! They *connived* to emasculate the greatness of his strutting essence. Somewhere, they had access to a service that guided them to their appointed mates, aligned their pelvises to precision collision with that pre-determined, pre-destined Other. He handled his genitals and moaned in despair, like a benthic creature unraveling in the shallows.

How many times had they "checked" to see? Weighed him in those scales, appraising? And again and again, that Belshazzarian disappointment, as gleefully they paired one to another into sweet couplings, held at intimate distance. They matched, as precisely as Caleb's images locked into the clicking sea outside. Never had he known a union, so achieved, to fail, and never had he heard of matrimony otherwise conceived.

Given the perfection of the company's advertising campaign rivaled that of this fatal woman-denying mechanism, Caleb was surprised when George marched into the office, the very picture of displeasure. The drafts for the new project had not gone over well, and the executive seemed quite animated in his unhappiness. "No," he said. His face looked like a bowl of bulbous, unhappy oatmeal. "No."

It was unusual for George to come down to the workshops.

He huffed forward, dopplering on in a field of breathing and frustrated shoe noises. On a table in the middle of the room he planted a small projector, and cast the draft in its current state on the wall. In three glimmering dimensions, the Holy Land stood pinned between a glistening quarter-pounder and something that might have been cesium. Below that came the title of the project and, further down, Jesus scored a touchdown, rags flapping as he punched through a cavernous hole in the collapsing line. Something was wrong.

"We have a way of doing things here at Longshot," he said to the room at large as everyone turned toward him. "*This* is not it. We are careful: we show care. In the precision of our execution lies the greatness of our work. We translate, formlessly, from desire to reality. They don't know they want it, we know they want it, we make them know they want it, and then we let them have it!" He started suddenly upright, as if struck by the simplicity of the point he was making. "That's it! Anything else, anything beyond this, is not only unnecessary, it is *fatal*." He made an emphatic gesture. Mona had swiveled around on her stool to watch him, her tiny hiney punched into the cushion and her weight way back. She maintained her balance by grasping the far end of the desk across her body so that the whole of the workspace was visible as she took in the harangue. Her eyebrows startled up her forehead. "Do you not understand? This has never, ever been a problem but now – I find – at this most critical moment, that you are prepared to desert me. Will I be undone? You seem to seek to undo me. And I do not know why. Look at this!"

The tone of his voice indicated that he was about to raise a hand to his brow, but he did not. It was true that something seemed off; Caleb, looking at the image, did not feel the traditional impulse to consume that usually accompanied the first encounter with his office's finished product. The room was silent. Caleb's eyes drifted from the image to rudder about the workspace; he found himself attracted to a little flash of color in the corner of Mona's screen. He squinted to focus on it. It looked like one of Vera's messages? She raised her arm a little and blocked his view. Perhaps she had been preserving the janitor's communication as well… He had kept them himself and stared at them hourly to cultivate his seething bile. The fact that she had remained there was irksome to him, in many ways.

"But that's it!" George continued, animating

again. "That's it! Just *do* your job, like you've *done* your job before, and I won't ask *another* thing in the world." His tone lifted a little, became warm. "Let's do this. Let's do this together, but let's all do our own part. Okay?"

That seemed to end the speech and there was uncertainty, followed by an unrealized opportunity for light applause. George turned to busy himself with the projector and Caleb was favored with a final glimpse of the draft. There was something in the Savior's eyes, a tangible something, as he charged into the end zone. The hole in the line gaped like the cavern when the stone was rolled away – that had been the trope – and Christ rocketed towards the viewer, reaching forward with a single, stigmatized hand. His face was flushed red, deeply red, the veins a-pulse with warm, intoxicating fluid. Caleb thought of all that wine and his mouth flooded again with the juices of anticipation. The image made him want something, but it didn't seem to be Microinsurance. The power cut and the montage vanished.

"Caleb, could I see you outside?" George asked as he packed up the projector.

Caleb followed him.

"Look, could you tell what was wrong with it?" George asked. "I couldn't put a finger on it myself but there was something, something I knew that wasn't right. Look. Here, uh... take this." He pressed something into Caleb's hand. "There's a lot of money on there. You're the manager now. Take the team up to the amusements for a while, for bowling or something. Have them watch a few movies. I don't want anyone to take a crack at this again until they've all had a chance to clear their heads, okay?"

Caleb met his eyes. He must be The Manager. "Okay."

"Good. Go to it then," and he turned to leave. "Until the end of the work day should do it. I imagine those trends will still be valid when you get back to work." Then he left.

Caleb looked down at the object that had been pressed into his palm: it was a card for the Executive Entertainment Center (EEC) near the building's peak. George usually found an excuse to bring the company up there once or twice a year for team-building activities wherein Caleb felt the transparent vacuum between himself and his co-workers more keenly than ever as he tried to focus on racking up points at pinball. Going up there was supposed to be a treat and was, in theory, popular with the staff. At least the card was shiny. So shiny! He stooped over it and examined closely his lower gumline in the reflective surface. Appreciation for the quality of his oral health purred within him, rolling over on itself. He made sucking noises with his lips and thought about Jesus's face as a fraction of his own looked back at him. The card then went in his pocket and he returned to the office to gather everyone together for the outing. There were five of them: Mona; the cousin of Sophie's, who shared none of her majestic, physiological blessings; two other graphic designers – twins, whom he never addressed directly for fear of getting their names confused; and the newly-arrived intern. Ladies all and doubtless so, each and every one of them.

He clapped his hands and they gathered around him in a widely-spaced semi-circle. He lay out one-two-three the intent of the remainder of the workday. Everybody nodded and he led them out in a line to the elevator. It arrived and they entered. Work had been left where it was, back in the office. They all swayed in unison as the capsule accelerated upward. Caleb's ears popped.

The doors opened. Outside the entire floor was dark; not a light was on. Lamps inside the elevator cast a weak-willed luminescence over the threshold, which suffocated meekly into the emptiness, and that was it. Caleb knew that the room was gigantic, that it occupied the entire floor, but this could not be seen at the moment.

"I'll get the light," said someone behind him.

"No, let me," said Mona.

"Here, I can do it." That was the young voice of the intern. There was an impatient edge to it. Something rustled in the back.

Caleb reached out his hand and touched the switch. It was strange, he thought, for there to be friction among his co-workers like this. Every light in the cavernous room inhaled at once and illuminated. The effect was like a single, powerful lamp turned on over a painting in a darkened gallery; perspective clicked on and the expanse of the installation became visible. They were standing in the far corner of an acreage of entertainment, where video arcades, miniature golf, slots, automatic craps – pleasures and diversions of all kinds – were arrayed and on display, for review. The elevator discharged them into a slightly raised space and they gazed out over the breadth of the hall for a moment.

"Bowling," Caleb said, directing everyone. "We're going bowling," and they descended as a crowd.

He had chosen bowling deliberately – and not based solely on George's recommendation – before he called everyone together. As he understood it, the sole purpose of the afternoon and evening's diversion was to permit the easy passage of time, allowing the ladies' inner worlds a breather to cycle and purge themselves, before the weekend kicked off. Over three days, he hoped Israel would still be there and the cheeseburger would remain a cheeseburger. Or something similar. Bowling was just an ordered, time-consuming activity that guaranteed the concentration of all participants in a single place where oversight would be easy. Above his head he held his hand, inviting the rest of the team to follow him.

The lanes were pleasant: gutter-flanked rolling spaces leading to distant formations of pins, all well-lit, and, at the players' end, a control console on an island in the middle of a scallop shell of seats. Caleb chose one and dropped George's card into the proper slot; it ticked into place and the little machine behind the intake port hummed. He slowly traced the recessed outline of the receptacle with his thumbnail while this happened. Warm. He could tell the mechanism was warm behind the shining plate, and he lay his hand on its carapace. Everyone's historical scores and rankings popped up on the boards overhead and the girls filed into the space behind him.

And then they were bowling. Balls glided pinward on a schedule, smooth and easy as mercury on oil. After a few rounds, a routine developed of bowl-sit-talk-stand-bowl-sit-talk-stand and the space at the end of the alley was filled with regular noise in the otherwise empty hall. Whatever tension had been in the group that Caleb felt he'd sensed in the elevator appeared to have dissipated and everyone cycled through their turns at the pitch. It looked like they were all playing at their usual level, which meant that Caleb was losing horribly. But was this not, in a way, good? Did this not afford him an opportunity to display humility and to showcase, perhaps bashfully, his human imperfections in the face of his subordinates? Yes. Of course it did, yes. Indeed, he saw in his own performance confirmation of his elevated state — his command — as The Manager, and he threw gutter balls with poise enough to claim charm. Mona, still in her work shoes, was delivering a lot of strikes. He mused, seated. They were all fine specimens, he considered, all of them fine-sculpted things sheathed in comely raiment. Weren't they now? The twins had brought their workout clothes and were now decked out in matching gym suits, which he found very attractive to his eye as their supple limbs pinwheeled, pitching spares. Caleb turned to address the intern as she seated herself after finishing her frame, feeling lewd and avuncular. He turned his eyes on her and oped his mouth, a universe of possibilities awaiting.

"I…"

He was interrupted!

"Gah!" Mona ejaculated from the head of the lane, the exclamation aligned with a pop like God's knuckle cracking as the ball coupled hard with the gutter. "Hrn!" and before Caleb could lift his head, a cumulus of sounds like scattered building blocks popcorned off his eardrum. Looking up, he found that she had twisted an ankle and pitched a face-plant right into the wood; the orb had spun off, ungoverned, into the next lane and drained harmlessly away. Mona was making starfish spasms and trying to reorient herself. Above, her score this turn was faithfully recorded and the chart of her performance took its own right-angle nose-dive, ruining the continuity of her record. A tiny red light began to pulse in haste. Caleb rose from his chair and hurried over to her. He put his palm to her shin, felt her, lay his hand on her ankle to test its integrity. His words were kind and commanding. "You'll be okay," he said. He was The Manager. The other ladies fluttered in excitement, assisting in little ways. Mona, somewhat perspired, rose to her feet and was helped to a chair. Her person was uninjured, but she had left a painful streak on the wood.

"Let me get that for you," murmured Caleb, dulcet and low, and unbuckled her booties as Mona squirmed in the chair with her legs out. He fondled her calf and ankle heavily as he did so, exploring her epidermis. Oh, fascinating contoured curves and hidden places! Her toes were painted with stars, he found. Little white dots in deep black fields.

"I, uh… I…," Mona was breathing. One twin fanned her, the other held her hand. The intern ran for water and Sophia's cousin soothed her shoulders and her neck. Everyone was industrious in their tasks and the heat in the space rose with the handling and the healing of poor, afflicted Mona. "I'm…," she managed. "I think I'm, I'm fine."

"Here!" the intern charged back. "I couldn't find a cup!" Her palms were pressed together and she carried water in her hands.

Mona nosed in and drank. Caleb felt her toes relax and expand in his grasp, blood flushing to the pads of her feet. "Oh," she says. "I feel better." Everyone buzzes. "I think I'll be okay now." Caleb can feel her heart tapping in her heel. "I think I'll be okay now," he had heard her say.

She rose and padded over to the rack where the balls were arrayed. She plucked one from the bunch and cast it down the alley, watched it curve towards the pins and impact.

"I'm okay," she said. She turned and rose on her toes to lift herself just free of the ground. "I'll be fine. Let's play. Let's keep playing." Her tone made Caleb feel uneasy, in a small way; she did not sound like someone who is being managed. He clasped his hands and furrowed his brow.

One of the twins came next. She posed with the ball, poised, and just as she was about to make her delivery, stuttered to a stop. Her sneaker-tips had come to a halt just inches short of the line, with a whispering friction.

"Me, too," she said, and kicked off her shoes. Then she bowled and walked back.

The other twin took her turn, then the intern, then it was Caleb's time to stand at the fore. He took his shot, noted it, then turned to walk back to the girls and the chitter of their chatter. They were all now unshod, hooves a-twinkle in the lamplight. Legs, their legs were everywhere, all in a circle, tapping, swaying, turning. Their talk was incense in the air; he could not keep his ears open and maintain focus. They bowled out of turn and did not listen to his correction or direction. He stood, played, and sat as he should, but clung alone to protocol. And the smell of them! Frames bled together and the ladies perspired, musking over the assembly: they were beautiful things that smelled like the young of animals and their breaths were hot and meaty. Caleb's toes curled and groped at leather.

He felt peculiarly upright when he rolled and his game did not improve, though he did not sense it degrading, either. Unnoticed, he kept playing his part, trying to do his job.

When he stood to face another frame, one of the women complained of the glare from the console-top display. It shone in their eyes. Could it be turned down? Of course it could. He lowered himself to dim the screen and then clicked his way up to the line, walking a wire, where he drew his proper sphere and with it did what he was meant to do. The results were what they were. On turning back he found that, with the counter monitor dimmed, he could no longer see anyone's faces, but an overhead fixture cast light over the center, where their extremities protruded in a semi-circle, hemming in the middle. Their nude toes rippled like anemone in time with the wash of water that runs on the sand under the sun in the spring, when it's warm, and their talk reaches him like the straining surf. And, then, he recalled how:

Old Ocean rides
Upon all sides
Of that small reach
Upon the beach
Where He stands in the tides.

Caleb perched alongside them. He felt like a little animal, fearful of the shadow. His own knees shook.

5

The weekend passed, not easily for Caleb. He was tickled by constant anxieties over the two-day break and rest did not renew him. Images from his bowling with the ladies clove in his mind, a relentless distraction. He had the persistent phantom sense of feathers on his palms, agitating back and forth, the sort of irritation that made him want to ball his hands into fists, push his nails into his skin. His mind itched with recollection, a persistent rash on the inside of his skull. He slept not well at all and the drugs were no help; tossing and turning, he repeatedly interrupted himself in his dreaming.

But dressing on Monday pleased him. He ordered his hair, he clad his body, and then did fastidious things to his fingernails to ensure hygiene and ward off illness. Upon consideration, he even opted to tweeze his chest hair a little, shaping that tiny pectoral lozenge just enough to give him the quiet confidence, the delicate edge he needed to ensure success, today. Was it too much? It was not. Caleb snugged into his too-tight pants and set out. Desiring to send a message, he also arrived early at work, first in the office, well before anyone else would be in. The room was silent all over and calm as the surface of a drum. Clean, too: so clean he could hear his footsteps sounding in the high corners of the ceiling. He seated himself at his desk; it had been rotated to face the center of the chamber since his promotion, to permit him better oversight of the staff. Yet the perspective did not satisfy him. He got out of the seat and then scrunched down to fiddle with ankle-height knobs and screws, elevating the work surface incrementally. In the end, he managed to raise both throne and altar by about four inches. Four whole inches! He felt like he owned the place. Hiking his butt, he perched delicately on the chair's rim and then glowered over the empty space: he commanded respect, inspired awe from imagined clerical succubi, hushing them into productive silence. How great a difference four inches made, he thought, and how readily we overlook the possibility of perfection, in the details, where the Devil truly lies. Ooooohh... He smirked and maintained his pose of gaunt authority over his desk, in place, until the ladies arrived. Awkwardly, he was obliged to wait for half an hour, crooked like a rook and waiting, until the first of them bothered to show. Nevertheless, as each one entered he settled her in her place with a lidless, baleful glare.

The day began. Knowing that administrative details would take up a good portion of the morning, Caleb allowed himself a furtive survey of the trending marks for the new week. It relieved him to see that Old George's intuition had been correct and that the world was still contentedly focused on both the miracle of the Lord's rising and the sports gear alike. If the team had been recalibrated to perform according to doctrine, then honors awaited from up on high. O, fair renown and recognition! He did so love the smell of bay leaves, when it threaded lightly through his hair.

No one – nobody – in the office had seemed much awed by the elevation of his command station to its new height. This surprised him. Groping for an explanation of their behavior, he reasoned that the earliness of the hour might be playing a role. "The poor dears," he thought, "their senses are probably dulled from having only just risen. Fatigue is still with them. I will have to take the initiative to draw their attention to myself, and then the effect should become pronounced." But it had to be natural. He'd been granted supervisory privileges in the office management system, which permitted him to view everyone else's work as they were doing it. He began scanning the employees' efforts and within ten minutes he had discovered a minor violation: the intern was working on one of her developmental pieces and using colors in a range that was too saturated, beyond the levels permitted for the project. One does not use red like that! Oh, no no no no… Obviously, she was having trouble parsing the technical specifications presented in the design document.

She was here to learn; it was his duty to intervene. He issued a gruff, stentorian sort of noise and called her over. She rose. The room was hushed in concentration as her crisp, pointed mincing brought her over to face him.

"Here, you're doing this wrong," he said, and he showed her. "It's not to spec." Her eyes clicked up and down, back and forth, as she followed him in explanation. There was a sort of measured limitation in the work he needed to make her grasp. He led her tenderly through the steps of exegesis that transformed lifeless vision in to definite, alluring form. Their interaction was abbreviated and technical.

"I understand this now," she said.

The definition in her words touched Caleb inwardly, as if a beam of sunshine had softly parted his ribs to reach in and handle his heart and inner organs. Technique had been imparted and he felt blessed to have been the agent of its transmission; she'd responded to his authority. He softly bade her return to her desk and off she went to do good work for Longshot, just as the Radiant Founder would have liked. Her form was good, too, and he allowed himself a stolen moment of appreciation, ever so hasty, just enough to take in the angles. They were nice, so very nice, though he had but thread-width of time to relish them. Perhaps it was for the best? Her dress was an abrupt Chartreuse color, and he could not have dwelt on it without ultimately experiencing intestinal discomfort.

Once she'd settled herself back in her chair, he permitted his eyes a victory lap around the room, a tour of the realm of his dominion, for confirmation of his virile command. He saw no obvious sign of it... The old manager, before his unfortunate accident, had been a sclerotic disciplinarian and quite aged in spite of his youthful appearance. He'd had this powerful cough that had scared Caleb white when it barked unexpectedly behind him. This, he now recognized, was a sign of power, a puissant act of dominance.

In imitation, he made a horrible, racking noise. Build up, execution, and dismount were all intense, like the suffering of nuts and bolts in a live food processor. His trachea and esophagus spasmed dramatically, then were still.

But what was the impact? He began to trace again a constellation about the starlets in the room with his eyes, expecting to find them snapped rigid to attention. He placed his hands wide on the surface before him in the attitude of an autocrat, a fascist, his helmet pushed back, surveying troops. The first two were fine, completely to spec, and his gaze rested on them only briefly. But then he came to Mona and found her, to his surprise, turned towards him.

Impudence! Her face was trained on his in overt focus, the mouth just open and an open heat communicated across the space that stretched between them. Her lips and eyes had been painted with bold colors – almost totemic – as she focused on him. The intervening air seemed to act as a lens that magnified her smoking stare and heightened his unease. A singeing prickle crept over him as he met her eyes; he cringed, withered away, then rose and tried to meet them once more. He drew his arms in close about himself in a protective posture, disordering his workplace as he did so, and shifted his weight reflexively onto one haunch, back again away from her. When she turned away from him, his nostrils were dilated as if assaulted by the whiff of some unpleasant odor.

His reason returned a moment later and it was clear to him that his subtle stratagem to reestablish influence and win power over the staff had failed. Everyone was still working, with their backs turned to him; he wondered where the failure could have crept in. He relaxed a little and abandoned the dead insect pose. What could have happened? He ticked off the elements that his training, acumen, judgment, and discerning nature told him were key to establishment of unassailable authority. He pondered and dwelt over each one as it came to him, savoring its scents, feeling it in his mouth – and could find not one of them missing. He brooded and mulled. As far as he could tell, everything was aligned.

His consternation growled and, as it did so, he realized that his feet didn't touch the floor. Unconsciously, he had been dandling his tiny toes a finger's width above the carpet, in childish, carefree circles. The chair had been raised too high! How infantile he must have looked to all of them, all the girls, like a squalling babe with his nappies reeking!

"Ack!" he chirped and started his buttocks from the seat. When he landed, the raised desktop came level with the bottom of his sternum; the diminished fraction of his torso that was visible suggested dwarfish impotence. Oh, woe! Oh, vulgarity! "Gak!" He sidestepped. The furnace eyes of the females were on him now, now that he had leapt free of his post. They swiveled in their seats to point their bared knees towards him, attention turned on. Something needed to happen.

"You! All of you!" Caleb called, taking a step forward into the middle of the room. He had no idea what was going to happen. At this point, he was groping: trying to massage the flight instinct into something with charm that would land him back in his coworkers good graces. He took a further step forward and struck a little pose, as if trying to balance a peacock's giant majesty. It looked, to him, as if he had decided to make a speech? A motivational one. He was running on his brain stem. "Do you not know the importance, the impact of what we have been called on to do?

The gravity of it? This is change, people! No, not change… Development! Evolution! Say the word with me: 'Evolution!'" He raised his hands to them to reinforce inspiration. It was like trying to make a plant blink. They leaned towards him a little bit, but remained passive.

"Evolution!" he called again as more of his brains sparked on. "We are reorienting, the entire company is on a pivot and there's static in the air, a charge that lifts the hair and orients us, in parallel, towards the goal. And do you not see that in any realignment there is a leading edge, whistling to part the air, and that we are sitting on – no, we *are* – that blade? Its very point? Don't you remember what it says in the company hymn?

> Fear not the seas nor the wastes,
> For certain there is a way onward...

"*Here* we are. *This* is us. And we are marching, your shoulder an inch from hers, one leg kicking in time with another. We know our destination: Microinsurance. Perhaps we will meet the enemy, whose serpentine coils rope across our prize. Fear not!" No one was in the least bit scared: his audience stared back like freeze-dried fish. Lightning began to crackle between his hemispheres. "Our path is true and our resolve flashes golden in the sun!"

At this point, Caleb was transported. His eyes

saw nothing. What appeared to his mind instead was a blank tableau, an abstract field. The girls registered as color-coded roundels in space and he was above them, a bold quadrangle, above whom even higher daemons turned. From his eyrie, branching rays of influence forked down in darkened bolts across the vacuum, towards the ladies. As he spoke, he imagined blackened arrowheads piercing their tenuous membranes and anchoring in those pale interiors to reside in command.

"*You!*" He cast a finger at one of the twins, isolating her in his attention. "Don't you perceive the import of all this?"

The twin, boxed in her chair, appeared patient.

"*Last* time…" he paced and raved. The heat was in his skull now. "Friday. Friday! *That* was a failure. *Today* will be different. Today will be all about process and the organization of our effort. Think of it this way. George! He is the sun: he gives light. And I and the design documents are the atmosphere, which acts as an optic to focus and filter that radiance so that it can be utilized by you, the producers, the fertile life of the warm, good earth. Without his sun there would be darkness and without my temperate interposition your soil would be blasted into rock. Each step, in its order, is necessary. Do you hear?" He realized now that he was starting to make the same points that George himself had made on Friday and felt his nerves begin to cool.

He lowered his voice. "Each step, in its order, is necessary," he repeated. "And in acquiescence, in subordination, comes the majesty of our final endeavor, has not precedent in nature, nor in artifice either. Is it not clear? Please, permit to remind you, in closing, of the next line:

> Higher and higher, strain for the sun:
> Father, giver of glory.

He pumped his palms together, kneaded them, and scanned the crew. He smiled broadly, a million dollars high, a smile that reached his phosphorescent cheeks and lifted them like golden waves. What a recovery it had been, what a motivational experience, and built out of nothing but need and the moment.

When it became clear that the impassioned rhesis had concluded, the women turned to one another. A conference of glances and half-syllables followed, then one of the twins – the other one – straightened up and said:

"Actually, we've already finished the project. Mona got us all to come in over the weekend and rework it from scratch."

Could it be? He deflated a little. "Is this true?" he asked, addressing, directly, the mastermind.

"Yes," she said. "We all pushed through Saturday to get it done." Everyone's head started bobbing. "I even took the initiative to have the proofs loaded in frames for display, so they're here for you to look at and correct."

"Then, where are they?" he asked someone else.

The intern volunteered to respond. "I put them in the closet over there," she said, and pointed to a space behind Caleb's desk, where a small panel was outlined into the wall. "Oh…"

Uncertainty snared him again, as if he'd just given the whole of his declamation to an audience whose respect he had not doubted, only to find in his finishing lines that his pants were on backwards and a graceful dismount impossible. Years ago, after the first round of layoffs, he'd seen something similar happen during the severance speech. Unwilling to receive their termination with Yoon's equanimity, the eliminated staff had gotten into the air purification system and swapped out the original, pleasant scent the building favored for something that smelled like a slaughterhouse, then timed it to release when the keynote speaker rose to the podium. She'd started bravely, but by the time she was five minutes in the whole theater stank and the inconveniently vegetarian orator had puked like a horse. After that, she'd staggered miserably off stage and the event had, on that note, precipitously concluded. Caleb self-consciously turned his back on the team and circled his workspace to come to the closet where the intern claimed the drafts were stashed. He had the self-control to place one foot before the other and not shake at the knees; with each step he seemed to be side-stepping that unfortunate lady's vomit by a precision inch or less.

Arriving at the portal, he turned to look back at the females. They had risen from their chairs and stood facing him, an uneven phalanx of bosomy effigies, mute. The door, before which he now stood, did not come up to his full height and he had to bend at the waist to reach the old-fashioned handle, which he turned to open. Inside, it was inky-black. He waved his hand before him, hoping for a sensor-activated light; the dark remained unchanged. At this point he might have stopped and tried to reason his way out, but fear and obligation pressed him forward and swung his leg over the threshold, into the shadowy interior.

Inside, it was very quiet. Other than the outline of his shadow hunched in the doorframe's enclosure, he could see almost nothing. He drew his other foot into the room behind him and, still hunkered down, extended his hands and fingers forward, tenderly making circles in the air, hoping to collide with something. There was nothing. Tenderly, he took two more fruitless steps deeper into the sanctuary. With his arms outstretched and his legs bent as they were, he looked absurdly as if he were balancing to lay an uncomfortable egg. It was ridiculous; he sighed and permitted his emotions to relax. This was not the way forward. A fool he might look scrabbling back to his coworkers standing outside, empty-handed, but a fool it seemed he would have to be.

It surprised him to find his way out barred by a brace of female torsos and legs. They were all barefoot again and fifty toes – painted and nude – were pointed his way. His co-workers must have all kicked off their shoes and padded silently over after him. Of their faces he could see nothing: the wall above the low frame interposed between Caleb's eyes and theirs. They stood in a brace, immobile, and yet alive all over with tiny twitches, weight readjustments, light rockings on ankles. To him, it was not so easy to tell who was who, which was which.

"Um," he managed, sounding little like a hegemon. "Hello?"

A whisper whispered in his ear, gently: the susurration of the heating system trying to warm the workspace, still a bit too cold in the early morning. Otherwise, the only other audible thing was the tactile action of bare toes working the floorboards.

When they closed the door on him, it was only a continuation of almost-silence. The band of his vision simply narrowed – the darkness serially consuming standing legs – until it was reduced to a slender ribbon, a single floss of fine light, and then it clicked away. Just before that singularity and the total loss of illumination, Caleb had a feeling perhaps similar to that his unfortunate heiress had had, that day on the tarmac when she beheld the purring maw of the engine and briefly known that she probably wouldn't be getting her livestock back again. He did not panic, though that seemed like the natural response. Unable to see a thing, even the faintest detail, he turned to press an ear to the door and listened to the activity outside.

There was a shuffle, a crab-like scuttling over dry terrain dispersing omni-directionally, then reforming somewhere else in the room. Voices followed as a distant gush to patter down hill in a rill and fill the space in Caleb's closet as he presses harder against the door and tries to make out the character of their conference. Heat loads the air between the crowded syllables, packed so densely, and the only thing that he can make out is their tempo carrying on upward, higher and higher, in a mounting cadence. Outside, something is exciting.

"Oh!" someone calls out. "She's sent another one! Come see!"

Footfalls course to a corner of the office and then there is the silence of serious consultation. After an indecipherable pause, the sound of human steps comes again, measured now. Heels are falling as an orchestra that Caleb can feel in rotation. So strange, to him, it seems, and he presses even harder against the door, mashing his cheek and ear flat. The tempo rises slightly. Against this ascending, floor-struck beat that floats in circles upward, Caleb strains to hear an uncommon melody. He wants to hear one, wants to hear flute and tambourine among the stomping celebrants, *yearns* to. He wishes he were outside, with that music, if it is there. The cadence accelerates once more so that his listening ears grow dizzy and he starts to feel uneasy now, threatened by the urgency of their business. Voices emerge, clamoring all in vowels repeated as a sequence again and again, over and over, higher and higher until it gets to be too much and Caleb, warily concerned, shrinks an inch away from the door and commences a retreat into the depths of the closet. One faceless voice then rises above the others and he can hear her words:

His eyes take in the sun that dominates the air
In this, which is an arid land and bare.
The sands beneath those rays flash white
And radiate their solar might
Into His marine face
As he begins to pace
Inland. His steaming tracks His will declare:
"This! Which is an arid land and bare,
"My sacrament will soon proclaim!
"The buried seed will turn to grow,
"The spring long lost begin to flow.
"The seed to grow!
"The spring to flow!
"Life again will know its name."

Then they chant the chorus over again,

completely out of time, like a chattering swell of language pushing down and along the straitened banks of a small tributary, rolling onward, thundering towards catharsis and the open sea beyond. The turning words roil with gathering momentum, forcing Caleb farther from the door, into the chamber's secret recesses, and the unbridled womanhood of voices looms over him through sheet rock and plaster, threatening to overwhelm and press him into the earth. His heart beats so fast, rushing blood, pounding as in the veins of juvenile creation, straight to his extremities. The momentous wave of sound surges onward, broader, bolder, charged with furious energy, until finally it breaks in a florid spray upon an expanse of emptiness, and dissipates. Then the music stops. And with the ceasing of the music, Caleb fell. He crashed over unseen objects that trapped the ground behind him and landed hard on the space between his shoulders with his legs in the air. Outside, the raindrop step of his team pattered away into a range beyond hearing and he was in solitude. A wild uproar it had been, and then a numbed silence.

There is no good reason for a man to blink in the dark, but Caleb did so. Whereas before he had been unable to find a thing in the blackened crawl space, now objects rolled about as he gathered his person into composure. Metallic things, cloth things flopped and clattered in the trackless void.

He could see nothing: the world had simply absented itself to become invisible, which presented problems. His heart was suspended over an immeasurable blackness, as infinitely deep as the starless altitude above him. With an effort, he managed to stand and locate enough of his body to brush himself down, whereupon he found that he had become horribly disoriented and no longer knew where the door was.

"Mona!" he called out. "Anyone? Hello!" Two steps he took into the void, trying to advance manfully towards the perimeter and feel his way back, but his pants leg snagged on something and pulled him off balance. Forward he pitched, knocking his shin on the hard edge of something unseen and completely failing to cushion his fall with his hands. Caleb augered in like a sloppy pelican into a pile of stacked, rubbery things, which scattered on impact. He lay for a moment in the absence of all stimulation, blind, mute, numb, completely unaware. His existence was a kind of secret here, even from himself. In the deprivation of his senses – though unable to act – the freedom of a man unobserved bloomed in his horizontal bosom. Things done only by night, strange rites, seemed possible to him. Time did not even pass.

But he folded his arms into a position that afforded leverage and exploited mechanical advantage to free himself from the earth. Again erect, he envisioned the blank space before him sectioned into quadrants that could be procedurally bisected, reduced until he located the way out within one of them. There were only so many places the exit could be hiding, after all, if one was willing to section away the unknown. He approached the vacant face on quiet feet, threading his way with now apparent ease through the detritus on the floorboards, and felt his way along it. Measuring his way forward, he came to a corner, turned, and continued his progress along this line he had found for himself. It was easy now. He found a handle.

The vacant office opened to him. Stepping from the darkened cabinet into the well-lit room, it was not his eyesight that was overpowered by the change in the environment, but his sense of smell: a bloody, musky scent hung in the air, cut with herbs and grasses. The only sound he heard was the light. Caleb called for his coworkers – received no response. He batted his hand back and forth in front of his face as if to clear away the miasma, but to no result. Going to his desk, he retrieved a flask of scented fluid with a spritzer from one of the drawers and started making a circuit around the precinct of the place, dispensing cleansing puffs as he went.

He met their shoes at the entrance, where they had been left in a mingled heap. He saw stilettos paired with flats, matched with wedges, mixed with kitten-heeled mules… it was a clod of ladies' footwear. He prodded at the end of it with his right foot. The girls were obviously gone and he had no idea where they'd run off to or how to get them back.

Of greater interest was the display in Mona's hutch right next to him, which was still turned on. It caught the eye. In the foreground he saw the text of the poem he'd just heard chanted, written in that unmistakeable, multicolored font, but behind it another item peeped around the frame, trying to edge into view. From the title he could see that it was a draft of some sort, but of what? Feeling there was nothing better he could do with himself at the moment, he laid a finger on the screen and brought it forward.

A new picture filled the surface, with color and abstract, tortured forms, all green, blue, yellow, black, white, and orange. Curves sloped sinuously into each other to meet in vertices where shades of sumptuous crimson melted together, outlines forgotten. Sparks of azure, cracks of goldenrod energy wound rocketing about the frame. In spite of this profusion of color, Caleb's eye saw as little there as it had in the darkened room, moments before. There was no face to recognize here, no body, no sensible thing at all. Fields of form he saw, punctured by color-wells, and a shadowy crevasse on one side, impenetrably murky, but beneath that opaque haze he knew there lay nuggets of ruby, lapis, emerald, and sapphire. These twinkled under piled abstractions, heaped like boulders, and exhaled hot fumes in the thermal plumes of the gasping vents of the underworld: vapors of creosote, sulfur, iodine.

"This is what they have been working on?" thought Caleb. "This will *not* sell insurance," he concluded. He felt as if some fundamental law of Art had been violated. How right he was.

He pressed down on a sensitive space on the screen and the project disappeared. Would it be best to pursue his errant staff wherever they had gone, in the hope of retrieving them to return to work, to finish the job? He calculated. He had none of Mona's access to the company security systems and no clue as to where they might have run off to, assuming the group had remained whole as it traveled and not simply scattered. All he was capable of was marching at random from one hallway to another, the probability of his success halving itself – at best – with each intersection he encountered.

He mused on his still-fresh memory of the drawing, the horrible image those girls had made. It could have been done better, and well did he know it. Perhaps the project was still salvageable? The work required would be onerous if done alone, but he knew he had the technique to make it happen. He returned to his own station, adjusted the seat and work surface back downward, then loaded the drafts and tools he needed to do the job. Why not finish the thing, if they weren't going to do it? he asked himself. Well? Why not?

6

Occasional contrary impulses aside, Caleb was always relieved when he found that there was a process in place to accomplish something. It eased his mind to find a task reduced to a series of operations, as with cleaning his hair. Others – to their peril – may not pay close attention to the written instructions printed on the back of the shampoo bottle, but he always read them with assiduous focus. To him, the existence of a documented procedure indicated that there had been another rational mind that had gone before and lived to tell the tale. And, when considering the manifold dangers that he was certain to have side-stepped through careful compliance, he blessed himself. He saw that there was a sort of brutish appeal in a life lived ungoverned, but prudent restraint kept him distant from it. He disdained to be small-minded or dissolute and had long ago judged this personal distaste for such action to be among his more mature traits; that it bordered upon paranoia he revealed to no one. When balanced with that pity he felt for others who were not so fortunate as to share his state, his emotional bearing took on something of the coloring of a saint.

This feeling of alleviation at the unseen presence of some guiding hand came upon him most strongly in his work, now more than ever. Consider the magnitude of the task before him! The doing of the deed would have been baleful enough in itself, but now he had to face it alone, doing a job meant for six… without the operating manuals, he'd have been lost.

The assignment was important: it had to be done. Caleb took a moment to center himself and pacify his mind – purge it of interfering humors – before beginning. This was the prophase. He closed his eyes and evacuated air from his nose in harsh, metered bursts, driving away the lingering stink that hung about him; he was satisfied only when every trace of vegetable scent had been driven from his nasal passages. When he breathed in now, the taste was clean and pure as silver. He opened up again his eyes and was seated. Triage, now. Then planning. It was possible that he'd be able to start in on the main effort of production today, but that was far from certain. There was so much to do.

He did not know it – there was no way he could know – but the work he did today was meant not for the market as a whole, but a single person. A young lady, in fact, now in the full flower of her life, chosen at random and her name unknown. She was the test bed: Longshot had churned through the produce of her life, beginning with the earliest years. Experiences from her childhood were drawn from the archives to be analyzed in composition with the relevant portions of her parents', siblings', and neighbors' records. From a sparse start, the density of collected matter had mounted as she'd grown, and the dossier had expanded to compensate. Her illnesses and education were captured in high resolution, and the company had maintained on file positive proof of her earliest love, her first kiss, and so on. The volume was astounding. In the building's lowest levels, beneath the hollow halls of accounting, HR, and all the rest, her twenty-eight years of time on earth were strained through a silicon screen and fed into Caleb's lap as a deep-dive read-out on her various affinities for kittens, burritos, and airplanes. The things she liked. In the space of almost three decades, she had become a woman whose mind was highly titillated by the fuzzy honey bee and shiny, sterling jewelery.

The project requirements called for a full media blitz and Caleb delivered, though it took him days to finish. The office remained empty: his staff did not return; they burned their sick leave instead and did not come in. In the moments during which he realized they were gone, he preferred it, though their help would have been a boon. The task demanded much of him, but deadlines meant the effort had to be kept brief and did not permit it to expand to a miry, Assyrian length. His assault on it was focused and brutal. Clicking through the doctrine, he was unwittingly producing for her – this distant lady – the thing that would win her heart in a more intimate moment. Starting with still images, within a week he had pushed through to the dynamic video montage and custom scents that would complete the package. He lived on dispensed meals and went home only to sleep. Once the payload was complete, he loaded it for delivery and depressed the button. From all sides came the onslaught: the young miss was bombarded in a fusillade of advertising, completely overtaken; defenseless, she was stalked and assaulted at her every turn by the elements of his design. His combined barrage represented a coordinated effort against every separate thing that she considered central to herself, even those sensitive corners of personality she shared with no one. At the end of this punishing, surgical assault, she – unknown to him and time zones away – caved to the majesty of his offensive, threw open the gates of her city besieged, and succumbed to his ultimate thrust in a final, tapering gasp.

"I must," she breathed, "buy this insurance. I simply must. It was meant to be."

Back at the home office, Caleb received indicators that the campaign had been victorious and was relieved. Microinsurance had been successfully fielded. He generated a detailed write-up of the effort that showcased his contributions and denigrated those of his teammates by implication. When he submitted the document, some program somewhere mined it for keywords, forced them through an assessment protocol, and burped up a small sum of money and three days off as a reward. It even dispensed a little stuffed animal with the Longshot logo stitched across its abdomen. A tiny triumph.

But afterward, confusion set in. His staff remained stubbornly absent and, consequently, he had no one to manage. No one seemed interested in managing him either. For the gaps in life where there was no obvious path to follow, he had grown to rely on leadership to provide him with a bridge across those idle chasms. The project having been finished in the early morning of a Tuesday, by the late afternoon he was frazzled. Between checking his accounts for new tasking, he would sit and try to focus on something without really having anything on which to focus; it was like trying to throw away a boomerang. He developed an overabundance of directionless energy. His one nervous tick was to pass his hand through his hair on the right-hand side and, by the time lunch came, he had flattened half his coiffure into an ugly, sebaceous mat. The noon-time meal he ate like a snake and succeeded in making himself feel ill with a dry mouth and disordered digestion. He believed his breath smelled like eggs, which revulsed him. Not knowing what else to do about the situation, he started drinking water heavily in an effort to clear his palette. There was a cooler in his office and he journeyed back and forth from it to his desk, pausing between trips to sit and vacantly hope that something would happen. Finally, in the early afternoon, when he stood up he found that he needed the bathroom desperately. He whimpered like a small animal and crossed his paws over his quaking lower abdomen. His big eyes peeled wide in discomfort, beneath the asymmetric hairdo.

But now, at least, he knew what to do with himself; as his physical discomfort mounted, a spiritual sort of relief crept in to accompany. On balanced tiptoe he waddled around the office, shut off the lights, set up automated responses, and prepared it for a temporary shutdown in his absence. True, he would be gone for only a minute or two, but there was a way that things were done and this was it.

After completing the final draw-down and clicking off the illumination, he exited the office and was drawn up short by an unexpected flower. A sizable blossom lay near one of the interstices of the floor tile and somewhat off center, peeping up at him. The petals were all a dripping, intense red, deepening at the center to a forceful black, and dotted with sprightly flecks about its heart.

Quizzically, he stooped to reach for it and his bladder counter-struck in a menacing twitch. With a snap, he straightened; though it lay just at his feet, the bloom was out of reach. He whimpered again and shifted his weight back and forth on his feet before turning to surge towards the bathroom, at the hall's far end. Tears beaded in his eyes. The door flapped behind him.

Emerging from the facilities moments later, he was the picture of refreshment. In his step there was a jaunty spring and his crest had been realigned and then delicately tussled to give a calibrated twist of personality. He was re-buttoning his jacket on the way back to the office when he came across *another* flower, lain upon the floor. This one, however, had a footprint smashed across it and he judged that it had been trampled on his charge for the toilet. It was orange, unlike the other one, but of a color just as vibrant. He squatted down and did not pick up the thing, but handled its petals lightly where they were still fleshy and unbruised.

"It is cool and warm," he thought. "There is a weighty lightness to it."

He was crouched at a T-intersection. When he rose, he could see the door to his office, waiting for him, but to his right and down the corridor he spied another little mote of color. A yellow one. Should he investigate? He let the thought weigh, balancing it against the sense of disorientation and anxiety that surely awaited back at his desk, and he felt his legs stiffen and his heels dig in, ready to resist. And walking on to check out the next flower seemed more like work than sitting in an empty room, in a way. It almost *felt* like management. It really did, particularly the way the task fitted into a blank space in his will and drew him onward through it; he had set off down the hall and away from his office before his mind had even settled to rest.

Perfume welled in a dome above the flower and the fragrance was sweet, though he grimaced at it. He was fortunate to spot – at a distance beyond – another blossom at rest upon the tile; he was driven onward toward it. And, pleasantly, beyond it, around a corner, just in sight, another one lay. There was a trail of them, he found winding through the halls of Longshot, like a garland slowly scattered over a great interval or buds that had opened along a secret vine. He tugged in his breath as he passed each one and quickened his pace a little to hasten by, but he followed them nevertheless.

They led him onward to a closed door, which he opened and found a staircase that led both up and down.

A utility access? He was surprised it wasn't locked. Caleb was not accustomed to climbing stairs since the only places he ever went were connected conveniently by elevator. Furthermore, he firmly believed that lifting a leg that high off the ground could crease his trousers fatally; his typical gait was something of a low glide, with the soles barely airborne, skimming the floorboards. He drifted over to the railing that wrapped about the empty space at the middle of the structure and gazed upward: architecture vaulted above him, vanishing at a distant mathematical point, imperceptible in the altitude. The undressed concrete coiled like a snailshell above and relaxed in loosening ripples as it descended, around and round, tightening again below his feet. He tried to look down into the well of it and gasped as he was seized simultaneously at the neck and bowels by a commanding vertigo; it yanked him away from the banister and towards the wall before he could even really look down. He staggered backward. The second step he took in recoil was miscalculated and his fine leather sole landed unexpectedly on the stair below. Thrown off balance, he brought the other foot around in an attempt to regain equilibrium. As he lunged to recover, his inseam gave way dramatically.

"Rrrrah!"

Caleb clipped his legs together, bolt upright, rigid as a totem. All other discomfort forgotten, he probed the wound with his finger. The printed fabric of his intimates met his sensitive digits, between the dangling hems. How bad was it? What should he do? He found that the rent in his nethers was small, but placed at a vital point: chances were good that it would go unnoticed, if he could maintain proper forms and posture. Detection, however, promised the lasting shame of a vulgar reputation, and could not be discounted. Perhaps it would be best to return to his chambers right now and change? Several of his coworkers lived on the same floor as he did and, he realized, their being out of the office increased the likelihood of encountering them prowling about, doing whatever they were now wont to do. And yet, was the chance that one of them might return to the office greater? Risk and disaster clicked back and forth in his head, behind his eyes, like the beads of an abacus, clacking and smacking.

He was standing poised between stairs, when a sound came circling up the steps. Almost above or nearly below the level of his hearing, it twinkled just brightly enough to draw his attention and the mental sums he was playing with sublimated into an ether. He looked down the corkscrew staircase; indistinct, sussurous waves torqued upward along the gyring steps and crept on still to meet him. One step he took forward. Then another. He was marching now, drawn onward just as ineluctably as before, though differently. As he descended, he noted another of the flowers he'd seen before, waiting for him several floors below the last. Passing it, he orbited, again and again, at a fixed distance from the central shaft of air, working ever earthward, until at last a final floweret marked a green way out an open door and off to a hallway beyond.

The acoustics in the corridor were different and he could hear a human voice now, distinctly, but without character. He had entered the passage at a corner where the hall banked sharply and the contracted tableau before him was almost completely blank. Only one small area had any color to it: a tiny patch at the inside angle of the turn, right at the vertex. Crouching, he bent to examine it.

The wall was varnished to a finish so white and glossy that it was almost like tile; he could dimly discern his own outline reflected in it. But in this one small patch down by the runner, the treatment had been abraded forcefully away, so that the surface was roughened and a chalky powder caught in the nap of the rug below. In this space was a small design done in some foreign material, slightly moist and oily to the touch. It was a leaf. A leaf that stood on a vibrant stem, sketched in rough but suggestive detail. When he pulled his hand away from it, a chlorophyll suggestion clung to the hilly ridges of his fingerprints, so that the whorls stood out in definition. He held the colored tips to his face, near his nose: there was a smell. Maybe algal? Maybe mossy.

Peeking around the corner, he found a different world beyond. The rug had been shredded and pulled up in a diagonal slash that drove across the walkway and furrowed into the substrate all the way to the opposite wall, where the paneling had been clawed away and the surface scoured down again. All across this yard-wide path, someone had continued the floral design to a broader charge of green and flowers that erupted upward from baseboards to the ceiling at a slant, back across to the opposite wall, and then downward in a plunge to return to ground, a dozen meters further on. The passageway was long: the greenery made two and a half full loops before turning to the left, wending out of sight.

He entered the hall and took a dainty step over the florid path, his bloomers faintly flaring. Onward he walked, though it felt little like anything management would want now; in fact, it had become the sort of thing that seemed to require paperwork afterward. In the distance the sound continued and he was certain now that it was a human voice. Someone was singing.

The circling braid of foliage continued and he followed it on, past blue blossoms of the blushing shades.

It was like a tunnel some animal had bored into the building, without respect for the original architecture. He hadn't any idea where he was: probably somewhere above ground, but that was only a guess as there were no windows and all the office plaques had been defaced. Caleb, grateful that the overhead lights still functioned, peered into one of the vacant alcoves and found it as blankly anonymous as a skull without a face. It was possible that payroll had been here once, or the people who'd handled the hiring, but it could have been a statistician's office just as easily. Or maybe that of another, defunct graphic artist, much like himself? It could not be known. But outside, the transformed corridor seemed alive with a spirally, virally energy and a serpentine twist; it wanted almost to merit a name.

Round corner after corner he went, following the green, green ribbon, and the singing grew only louder. Notes, notes in the air, someone was passing him notes, quarter notes, eighth notes, a beat! He pursued. As he zeroed in on the emitting source, fidelity mounted, spiking to a peak, and he could hear the space for a face in the voice, see the features in it. A corner away from the singer's perch, he came to a stop and listened, leaning against a raw mural daubed with emerald verdure and indigo petals. With his ears open he huddled and attended and, finally, he heard the words:

> *"The buried seed will turn to grow,*
> *"The spring long lost begin to flow.*
> *"The seed to grow!*
> *"The spring to flow!*
> "Life *again will know its name"*

He was close now, so close as to hear the singer's movements, pounding, dragging, jumping. Her shuffle on the boards had texture now, all grainy woodlike; her toes pattered down on the arid flags. Caleb rounded the corner and it was Vera. She stood in what had become a cul-de-sac, though it had once probably been a reception area, in a previous life. Behind her, on the far wall, a sylvan efflorescence spread, tingling in color. Keys a-jingle at her waist, Caleb took a step closer: behind her ear a violet and her whole body in motion – her hair moves with her clothes and grooves with her limbs and proves nothing much at all. He took a step forward into her circle and she is spinning, a-turn, a-twirl, coming around for the impact, flask in hand. A moment from him she rises to a halt and her face is almost at him, but not quite. In her outstretched hand he can read the words printed on her hand-held bottle. Plainly declared, in juvenile capitals of every color, are the words:

BIG GOD WINE

"How florid," he thinks, "how florid all the little colors are." His eyes notice that the two Gs, placed closely together, are the same color. They're mauve.

"Will you drink?" she asks.

His hand is on the bottle and the bottle's in his palm. Closer he brings it to his face and then yet closer still… the cap is off and the fluid sloshes, promising him life. He sees again:

BIG GOD WINE

It is cool on his lips, but in his throat it's warm. Her face has so many colors, as he looks into it, doesn't it? In her eyes there is a hue that echoes in her lips and resonates in her cheek. She takes his hand. They, together, turn a circle, present with each other. His arms are all around her, up and down, and hers with him besides, as they are turning. The room is spinning; she smells like pandemonium in clover, myrtle, ivy, ash. What smell? A torrent of ecstatic scents, an insane din. Caleb focuses on her nose and eyes as the twist becomes intense and the entourage of color in the room drifts into a blur. With a wild uproar they pass into a space that's nameless, and all composure's shattered. He does not know where his legs are, where his arms are, or where they might be going. Her clothes are soft as fawnskin. Walls seem to fall and in that space he knows, he says:

"This never could end well."

Her teeth go in, where the shoulder's flesh. The life mystery of blood comes from him, into her open maw, ingested. He bellowed. She places hands about him, draws him in, close to the giving breast. A horrid slickness, wet, does spread beneath his garb – he turned, he pulled away. Tight are her jaws, compressing so, until the tooth meets tooth. He roared again and turned away, the wounded limb of the lamb a-drag and trailing.

Caleb ran; he broke in a rout. In a different rhythm his legs pounded up and down, hammering, as if a camshaft drove his limbs, and drove him away from the dead end chamber. Through the twisting hall he powered forward, all in flight, so fast that the color bleached from the world around him: he ran in white pain through the black helix, down which he'd come. He was carried through turns. The whole system of his lungs, blood, and muscle pulsed to generate propulsion, producing footfalls of acceleration. So hard he ran, and he pushed himself forward with such ill-directed vigor that, as he approached the exit to the offices that emerged into the stairwell, he could no longer lace his motions together and the windmill harmony of his limbs dissipated. Anything got in the way of everything all at once, just as he was reaching the upper limit of his speed, and as he came upon the landing he lost orientation. Caleb drifted off his center line and impacted with the door jamb as he failed to exit. His clavicle clove like porcelain. There was a click like a glass ampoule snicking open, and the pain poured in.

He rolled around the corner, the most horrible noises guttering in his larynx. His big, goat mouth was open, and it brayed. Two, three steps he staggered forward, blind as a mole in the sun. Slaver formed around his lips, drips of his pain water scattered on the floor. He made another horrible sound and tried to clutch at his wounds, but couldn't.

Caleb blacked out. When he woke up, he was in the clinic.

7

Caleb was unconscious when he arrived at the clinic. His need for medical attention was detected at the moment it occurred and he had been collected shortly thereafter, howling and foaming, only to lose consciousness en route. He'd awoken when some sort of mechanical scrubber activated and was applied to his face in an effort to scour away his streaming slobber. Reflexively he'd lunged to attack the whirling bristles with his teeth; medical disinfectants flooded his oral cavity and the wheel bucked in his jaws. Tranquilizers had coursed in then, tasteless pharmaceuticals, tuned to his body's weight and metabolic features. Caleb sagged and his jaw relaxed, then he drooled a little more. It was taken care of. He lay on his back, knowing not where he was, as things were done to him.

His experience was much like sleep. Movements fluttered along his body – through his fingers, under his eyelids – but purposeless. Syringes snuck beneath his skin and he did not feel them. How could he be aware of the thing that flowed and slowed the progress through his veins? The electricity in his extremities dampened to an inaudible gray. Gravity evaporated, and as it wafted away he too became a vapor, escaping into vacuum. In spite of his buoyancy, he sank, weaving on downward through openings slit in diaphanous fabric. Deep, at the bottom of everything, there was shapelessness.

There, in that void, Caleb wallowed. In his heart he felt at ease, secure, and supine, and yet it was as if he was on his feet in pale water that came up only to his ankles and the wind was almost chill.

His vision was very clear. He could see for miles.

Then the moonlit tide slowly rose about him and the earth beneath did shy away. In the translucent haze, the horizon absented itself and irregular mushrooms of color peeped in, winked out, all eyes of semi-understanding. He was surrounded. A tabor came up to him from deep down below, and the sounds of a chorus in motion, almost in time to the tapping of his heart. Deep, deep, deep, deep underneath, he divined the disjointed features of a face, down in the crush-depth, in the no-sun, the muscles behind it pumping insanely upward, firing onward, closer and closer until he can see the All of it together in One, and then the countenance dissolves and wings about him and past him like a cloud of fireflies, straining to be stars. He giggles as they rope between his fingers. Behind them trails a great sound bubble that swells from the bathic wells below, quivering. The whole thing vibrates through his frame, jiggling every organ, and hazes out his brains. A muteness passes. Then he hears behind his ears the color and he traces it with his mouth:

The infant green starts from its bed
At once; the curling tendrils spread
Across the waste, in sympathetic echo at His tread,
Much as the river mounts his dam:
The waters white, first, as the lamb,
As froth, as lace; but then the flood -
That roaring *excess* of the blood -
Erupting from the breach
As vines and trees and grasses each
Effuse to stain the lifeless sand.
All sprout and branch and strain,

Rising, rising, rising, rising,
Rising from the unmarked plain
To fruit and shade the land.
Creatures, emerging from the green,
Dart and repose, seen and unseen;
The lion, boar, the ugly ram,
And then that lamb – You are the Lamb.

You gambol near, seek cover from the rain.
His eyes are mad. His breath is warm.
He parts your skin and reaches in.
You give – the sapling in the storm,
The gasping votive to His sin.

Caleb's whole body is shaking under anaesthetic; he feels terror and gratitude only. Someone squats on his chest, eye to his eye, trying to show him something beneath the moon. There is a mask and a leafy beard with hanging, swinging acorns and branches that branch across space. Caleb's mind grasps the edges of its edges and pulls the breathtaking, unavoidable presence in. It swings upward before him, as if on hinges, and behind it is a vacant zone. He feels the future at play there. In curlicue space, he bends over to look down into the opening from the prone position. Whoever could have known that tomorrow lay there, beneath him, in a bowl in his lap? And flutes? There is, in music, a necessity for the function of time, which is a way to let the ripples of the moment propagate outward, across and through the waters. He reached for it and its dynamism seized in place to become a staring image; through the opening, he saw a moment. Then the whole thing was smothered by a dream.

A monochrome boundary traced its way around him, marking off a space for rest. Harmonious tones sounded off in the ringing air all about, with no obvious melody.

He turned his head and surveyed static fields of color. Before him he beheld luminous glorifications of drifting, geometric figures: a life-vanquishing beauty that overcame suffering loomed before him, ominous. The likenesses of things orbited, frozen in their perfect trajectories.

He breathed in; there was no air. His tongue was a dry finger that lay in his mouth. He parted his lips and probed the atmosphere with it – he felt the wind, and tasted nothing. Caleb's eyes opened.

Caleb awoke, confused. He pushed himself up on one elbow, sliding back in bed a bit to take in the room; his whole other arm was fixed in a rigid bandage with a brace that ran from his wrist to his collar and a wide bib that blocked his view of almost all of his body – only his distant, peeping toes were visible. The wall by his bed was one solid window and the sun beams advanced through it as a front to trace the outline of every visible thing. In addition to the ambient illumination, a surgical lamp reared up over Caleb's sickbed to light the whole of his unseen person, which felt nude under a gossamer tissue garment. He reached up around the edge of it with his unbound hand to seek a handle, found one, and cranked the filament away from him so that it pointed less in his face. "The joint moves so easily," Caleb half-thought to himself in hazy approbation. "It is pleasing to know the comfort of a well-lubricated bearing and quality machining, when one meets it." As his eyes adjusted to the lower, more natural level of light, he saw a backlit display hovering to one side, rolling text at him. He strained and squinted to see it.

The document was scrolling by very quickly, but it looked like a manifest of his treatment and condition. Trying to keep up, he picked out words and broken sentences, just enough to follow the gist of what was going on: unsurprisingly, a series of unfortunate technicalities had prevented his company-provided policy from covering a penny of his medical expenses. Instead, Longshot had nominated a sub-routine from the legal department to apply for power of attorney over him during the period of his unconsciousness, which it had received, and then sold the rights to his kidneys in an automated auction. Caleb didn't get the chance to see who had placed the winning bid – everything was moving so fast – but it looked like a shoe company owned his intestines now. A contractor for an experimental steel mill had purchased some other, indiscernible portion of his person, throwing down a startling sum delimited in an obscure currency to beat out an industrial pig farm. It dawned on Caleb that even his fingernails might now be the property of some foreign concern. He looked at them; they seemed no different. Turning back to the screen, he caught the fact that Longshot had shaved a shocking amount of money off the top of the total amount raised as overhead expenses and then paid itself the rest for the medical services rendered. In the end, it seemed he owed nothing but his various viscera, payable at the time of his future death, to sundry parties in private industry and government. There was a closing line:

Hark to the times and give ear:
O, look to the Order that's written.

He was then thanked for his hereafter legally binding acknowledgment of and assent to the terms heretofore mentioned, *mens sana* and all the rest. Of course, should he desire to decline or dispute the agreement – in whole or in any part – he need only place his thumb * here * before the timer ran out, and his non-acceptance would be duly registered with the authorities relevant to his case. Caleb lunged across his body and the inflexible cast to punch with his free finger at the interface and missed. The little bar was emptying rapidly. He strained –

"Ah, ah, ah!" said Old George, chastening him, as he drew the screen just out of reach. He'd been holding it.

Caleb looked up to meet his gaze: he had cobalt eyes with nitrate whites. Time ran out and the contract recorded his non-signature, then it winked away. His failure to dissent had been recorded as a success, somewhere else.

"There, there. Not so hard now, is it? Not hard at all." George flipped the tablet around so that it was perpendicular to the earth and then slotted it into a bag at the foot of his chair. "You're well?"

"I've been better." Caleb responded.

"You *are* better, far as I can tell."

"That's…" He let the sentence trail off. He was staring at the bag with the tablet in it.

No one said anything. Caleb's eyes wandered next to his barely visible toes, now a wholly owned subsidiary of an aspiring manufacturer of prophylactics.

"The office is well. You're needed back at the office," George offered.

Caleb told him that he was suffering from a major fracture and nausea.

"Well, yes. That's to be expected, I'd say, after what you've been through. It's unsurprising. But you'll be back."

"How long has it been?"

"A week. A little more. Nine days."

"Has anything happened?"

"Not much."

"Not much?"

"No. The system locked Vera's accounts after your incident so that she would no longer harass the staff with those messages of hers. Everyone was naturally drawn back to their posts after that. Work has returned to normal now."

"Naturally drawn back to their posts?"

"Yes. Naturally. Of course, *naturally*. How else could it be." George's voice was tinted with a delicate, almost melancholy reserve, a suggestion of superior knowledge. "Regardless," he went on, "regardless how it happened, everyone's back at their desks and the work's going forward. The project is a success: Microinsurance is being taken to the next level and your office bears most of the responsibility for that. You should be pleased."

Caleb, prone and bandaged, felt, indeed, that he should be proud.

"So I came to congratulate you. Naturally. And, naturally, you are aware that Vera is still here, in spite of your efforts?"

"I'd hoped she would leave on her own."

"She won't, though I concede that your earlier initiative to wait her out had a kind of charm. She must be made to go." He was final. "I have assigned an assistant to help you finish the task. She is here, too, at the moment, for a course of procedures of her own – reconstructive work – but will be soon discharged. You are going to accomplish the task with her help."

"Naturally."

George stared at him.

"I'm certain she'll be a great asset in the work going forward," Caleb continued. His voice felt strange in his throat as he spoke, as if his vocal cords had been surgically cut and then rebonded. He glanced up at the hanging tubes above him, the medical devices.

George rose. The interview was nearing its end. "Here," he said, as he fished in his bag and drew out the tablet again. He pecked at its surface. "You've played such a part in the rollout of Microinsurance; would you care to sample it?"

With one arm he extended the object towards Caleb's sickbed and let him handle it this time. It was heavy in his fingers, and cold. In his free hand he turned it about to look at the surface of the thing. It was so clean and shiny.

"It's a very representative policy," George assured him. "Very reasonable. We're starting with smaller, short-term plans to begin with and then advancing into bigger initiatives once we've staked a space in the market."

Caleb considered it: for a modest investment, Longshot offered to insure the balance of his sick leave at a certain level for the coming month. The total cost of coverage was less than one day of his labor, but the possible payout was immense. Sensing opportunity, Caleb pressed his thumb in the box and handed his acceptance of terms back to George. Injuries such as his demanded lengthy respite and his reserves were low; he was certain to collect.

"Thank you," George said, receiving the contract from him. "You'll be fine. You'll get the job done. Goodbye." Then he left.

Caleb lay on the bed. As he heard the sounds of George wandering off into the distance, his eyes faced forward and he thought. He thought vague thoughts.

Caleb lay in the nest of medicine and was cared for. With gauze, plaster, unguents, and technique, a line was plotted between the individual things that were his wounds, and the infectious world without. He was at ease: slithering tubes suctioned noxious spirits from him and reintroduced more purified fluids, and pain withdrew from the features of nature. Between his treatments there was little to do; he would lie abed and watch the various medical apparatus hurry about the rooms, grooming each other. With great solemnity, he witnessed a damaged arm removed from the device that provided his nutrients and the fusion of a replacement with numerous attendants in assistance. Caleb drank from tubes, ate from trays, and healed. The structure that held his arm in place was fastened to the headboard; it would not permit him to rise, so he slept often to make the time pass. He slept and dreamed. But when he woke he would see sometimes another figure, another patient, in the hallways, swathed in bandages and walking.

"Hie!" he called out, trying to get her attention; the figure was discernibly female – trimly, daintily so. He made plosive noises at her and vowels and nasals whenever he saw her from his pallet, but she did not respond and time passed.

Recovery was swift, so much so that it shocked Caleb to feel his body repair itself under superior ministrations. The fractured bridge of bone in his body reached out to itself and joined again. His swelling withdrew. For a grown man to recover from wounds as grave as Caleb's should have taken quite a stint of treatment, but with a juvenile energy he rebounded in only half that time. There was, however, one surprise that the clinic had lain in store for him: when his cast was sawn away and parted so that he could see his own limbs again, he found that his body had been stripped of hair. He tittered. Maybe they had sold it to a precious minerals exchange? Or a shoe shine factory? From the neck on down he was nude as glass and his legs flopped weakly before him. Over the space of his convalescence he had lost much strength. Later, as he piloted a toetip into his trousers, he found that they, too, had been healed. A delicate row of pink stitches fused the fissure he had wrought in them back on the stairs. Seated on the mattress edge, he slid them on. When he stood, over every inch of every surface of his shins and thighs and knees he could feel the whispering fabric in motion, twinkling on the fingertips of his nerves like dry, windblown leaves. He giggled when he walked. At least his shoes still fit.

Caleb made a faint effort to locate the other patient, then lost interest and shuffled home. He felt still somewhat unwell; not sick or injured in a morbid or traumatic sense, but occupied by the absence of health. Opening the door to his apartment, he found that something had been delivered to him during his convalescence. A box? Caleb lay down his things, took a knife from the kitchen, and incised into the packaging, laying open the top and exposing its insides. And what was inside? Bottles. Six bottles stood in separate cells, cordoned off by an insert used to keep them upright. He clamped one of them by the top with his fingers and elevated it out of its cradle. It was made of a recyclable material at a standard size, with a brightly colored label on it that said in what looked like handwritten letters:

BIG GOD WINE

He took another bottle from the box and held it alongside the first. It had the same label, the design of the lettering being so similar as to be an obvious copy. They all did. Caleb got a glass from the sink, cranked the top off one of them, poured himself a measure, and swallowed it. It was just plain, insipid water. The glass was sterilized and the mute color of the room passed through it effortlessly. He put the box away somewhere and spent the rest of the evening in his apartment, going to sleep when it got late.

He rose early, feeling unchanged. Dressing – usually so easy a task – troubled him this morning, as he could find few things that fit his narrowed dimensions. He had time, however, so he simply brute forced his way through the wardrobe with his weak little arms, clicking and clacking. Feet planted and hands in motion, he sorted, parsed, assessed, and finally chose a pair of slacks and a crisp, respectable shirt. Both articles of clothing went on the bed, lain as if on a human figure, so that he could step back and consider how they matched.

They went well together, he concluded. On his body, they were likely to project an air of expertise and efficiency. He put them on.

When he stepped outside and sealed his door, he still felt enervated, almost purged of something. But he took himself to the office, setting out at a purposeful stride: he aligned his hips, pumped his buttocks, and went into motion towards his goals, which he envisioned. His twitching eye saw for him the panorama of his workplace and counted the tables, counted the chairs, counted the light fixtures, wall hangings, and tiles on the floor. Images of every little thing in the office thronged in his mind and he channeled them to fill the empty spaces in his limbs. In the elevator, when he depressed the button to take him down to the level where he worked, Caleb started feeling much closer to recovery than when he'd left the clinic. Up and down he moved his reforged shoulder and it was perfect, seamlessly bonded. He stepped out of the opening doors into a new hallway and advanced like a solid object toward the chamber that awaited around corners and down corridors. His footsteps rang like the heralds of his powerful advent, of his reconquered health, now undeniable. Caleb was on his way!

By the time he reached the office, his step had a positive dynamism to it, his elegant, stripling limbs gently bearing him onward with a heron's poise and ease, dry above the surface of the water. From just outside, in the hallway, he could hear the familiar respiration of the workplace: the repositioning of human weight in chairs, the hiss and purr of idle chatter, the exhalations of the air purification system, combing away at the atmosphere. It was good to be back. As he was readying himself to enter – just as he was ready to enter – an eminence loomed into form behind the frosted glass. Was it Yoon? The outline was almost his; yet it made no sense for him to be there. Caleb wavered, on the verge of entering, uncertain in the hallway.

Then the door swung open and the situation resolved itself. It was Old George, once more.

"Good to see you, Caleb. So good to see you…" he said, extending a hand. Caleb took it. "And right on time, too. Right on time… I'm assuming, of course, that you've recovered and are coming back to work?"

"Naturally," he replied.

"Of course," George affirmed. "Ah, well. It's a pity you won't be collecting on that policy. Things came pretty close, I know, but rules are still rules. That's the way the world works."

Caleb nodded.

"You've got work to do now," the boss continued. "Let it happen." He maneuvered around Caleb and glided off, toward the elevators. Then he was gone again.

Caleb was in the office now. There were five desks in the office; five desks and two chairs and six lamps – of which four were ceiling-mounted and two were freestanding – and two, three, four prints of various scenes hanging on the walls and tiles set in a thirty-two by forty-eight grid, making a total of one thousand five hundred and thirty-six. He also counted only four people present, other than him: Mona, Sophie's cousin, and the twins.

"Is the intern sick?" he asked Mona, turning to face her.

"No, sir. Her time was up so she went back to the company school. A replacement's been assigned and her things brought over, but she's not started yet." There was an unwonted tone of respect in her voice, and Caleb appreciated it.

"Thank you," he returned. "Do we know who it is yet?"

"It will be the girl from down the hall. Her nameplate's on her desk. Excuse me, I have to work now," and Mona returned to her display. It looked to Caleb like she was editing code: the screen was full of black characters massed together in a bleached field of white. She raised her hands and started adding symbols and numbers to the bulk that was already there. Again, Caleb felt an upwelling of appreciation for her and this seemingly new, deferential behavior of hers; she really seemed to have turned a corner. He spoke to each of the twins and the cousin in turn and found them all pallid and submissive to his authority, prepared to respect him in his proper role as manager of the office. It was good. Then he strolled onward to the intern's vacant carrel and discovered two piles of belongings in unopened boxes, unmarked, stacked in symmetric towers at each end of the tabletop. The name sign Mona had mentioned stood between them, occupying the perfect center of the area, and on it was written:

SOPHIE

Caleb felt a jet of excited unease try to spurt up within him. "Ooooh," he mooned in a tiny voice as he remembered her shifting pillows of beckoning flesh, the absurd contours of her person – alluring and almost uncontainable. His teeth went out of alignment in his mouth and his hands went down to smooth and soothe the lower regions of his physique. "Ooooh…" Then his own self-image occurred to him and he saw himself, in his mind, as he might appear to the ladies of the office. This checked him. He recalibrated to assume a stance of willful composure and laid his fingers up about his lapels, tugged them tight. Turning back to Mona, he addressed her from halfway across the room.

"Mona, this is where the new girl sits? Sophie?"

"Yes, sir. *Will* sit. The machine dropped her things off two days ago, but she hasn't been in."

"This is Sophie from down the hall… Sophie from the travel department?"

"I believe so."

He turned to the cousin. "Is this the Sophie you're related to?"

"Yes, sir," she responded and twisted around to face him. She'd been designing a piece for one of their jewelery and precious metal policies, and her screen was lined with fulminating gold.

"Why didn't you tell me that it was her cousin that was coming down here? You must have known."

"I didn't want to imply any connection between anyone," Mona responded. "It wouldn't have been appropriate."

Caleb nodded; he had to concede that there was an air of impropriety about the whole thing and Mona's decision to withhold information reflected probity of a type. He inquired further if they knew when she would arrive and they did not, though it could be any day now. He strode back to his desk and assumed his station as their superior and advisor with a swish and a sway of swinging fabric. Was his weight loss having an effect? Whereas before his legs had hung impotently from the seat above, now they seemed buoyed up, carried from the floor's surface by a rising cushion of heated authority that touched at his toes, as his heels hovered in the free air. Once more, it felt good, oh so good. Just right.

For the next two weeks, work was a machine.

Caleb felt that he saw with a new clarity, commanding respect and action, as the ladies spun in their chairs and their fingers clacked on the work surfaces. Every day he looked at the numbers: the numbers were good, the numbers went up. Microinsurance was big and his office was driving the sales. Old George came by often now, smiles up to his eyes, with stories of resounding success. "Caleb," he said, "you're doing so well. I'm so proud of you." He fit his hand nicely over Caleb's shoulder and the younger man could feel the cool dryness of the older's palm through fabric of his coat. Work progressed. They insured only small things like a lady's hairdo for an evening or a carpet for the hour when the neighbors' animal was over. Nobody ever collected and it went well for them; there are so many tiny, granular worries in a life and each of them can be put to dreaming sleep with the assurance, the *comfort* that Longshot provided, all at rock-bottom rates, which was money in the bank.

At the beginning of the third week, Sophie arrived. How changed she was! She approached his desk, stone white, along a straight line at a regular pace. He saw that her irregularities were gone – her heavy, swaying glands had been scraped away and sewn artfully over, and someone had reset her teeth. In fact, the whole structure of her face had been completely overhauled, and her eyes met his levelly, evenly now. To Caleb, she looked a perfect type.

"My name is Caleb," he said as he rose and extended a hand, realizing too late that she certainly knew his name already. She slipped her nails through the space between his thumb and index finger. The reconstructive work covered the whole surface of her body.

"Hello. I have heard you will be my new manager. I am Sophie." In her voice there was a measured tone that prohibited excess and begged self-knowledge. They withdrew their hands together. She appeared totally self-aware and ready to take on any role, advancing directly to the limits of the permissible and going not a single step beyond.

"What miracles they work these days," thought Caleb. "What gracious gifts they give," and he dismissed her.

Sophie meshed noiselessly with the operations of the office and the engine turned as fast and faster than ever. Her comfort with the work fed Caleb's energy and guided his drive to direct; it pointed his hand, while he – in turn – nourished her with his synergistic feedback. She had been to all the best schools. Production soared. From his aerie, Caleb could compare her and Mona in comfort and analyze the distinguishing features between them. It was a poor contest for little Mona: alongside her new co-worker, she appeared lost and out of focus. Sophie's hands cranked and fired as she worked, running on dry heat and burning off a powerful, buried reactor, so that there was no contest. Accolades began to filter down from above, on high… and, by degrees, Caleb became aware of an inevitability. The thrown ball, lofted, follows helplessly the line drawn for it that marks the path to its destination, and his heart opened like a glove to receive it.

In the course of duties, it was to be expected that work would run sometimes late. Not that the entire office would remain at their desks past the time when they were due home, but just those one or two dedicated individuals who were reluctant to leave a task undone. Fatigued, they would finally turn to bed for rest and rejuvenation in quiet dream, and then return. Caleb had done this before; it was occasionally required of them all. And – in the course of duties – necessity demanded Sophie do the same. So, one evening, Caleb stayed with her, and they dined together.

They had remained at the office well past the typical dinner time and the cafeteria was almost deserted when they arrived, though it was starkly lit. He took his place and she took hers: they were facing each other, across the table, separated by a field of starched linen and cutlery that glittered like ornaments.

"This is nice," said Caleb.

"I agree," she said.

She looked as pleasing to Caleb as the meal did

when it came. He supped tonight on a steaming plate of colored rods, arranged with artifice in the center of his plate to form a dainty architecture. Her neck was a dainty architecture too, Caleb noticed, as he divided and subdivided and then carefully partook of his prepared repast. He considered the column of her anatomy on which her head rested and swayed, hewn and marbled with the finest veins, which communicated from the pediment of her forehead to a foundation buried beneath her collar bone. How perfect, how *just so* – nothing more or less than what was needed.

"It feels so good to be here," she declared. "The work is so important."

"It really is," he confirmed. "That's why George takes such an interest. It only makes sense."

"You think so?"

"Yes."

"You admire him?"

"That's…" he took a moment to fit his words together. "Yes. He is a model for us. For us all. And I think he remembers the reason why we were brought here and understands – is loyal to – the Founder's original vision."

"So do I."

He was glad that they agreed. Caleb pierced a colored morsel on his plate and elevated it to his mouth, self-assured. He squared the flavors on his tongue.

"You seem to understand it well yourself," she continued.

Caleb chewed.

"I suppose that's why you're the manager."

To Caleb, these words were succulent. He pulverized his food in his jaws and focused on his posture. The meal diminished and their conversation continued in an easy concatenation. Caleb grew voluble. True, they were not drinking, but he found there was a verve and a satisfaction to be had in the act of holding forth that slid lubricant between his senses, edging him towards monologue.

"I have such hope," he harangued. By this point he'd eaten exactly seventy-five percent of his meal and the remaining quarter occupied a sculpted wedge on his plate. Drawing on three weeks of managerial experience, he continued to speak. "George realized that uncertainty is not only exploitable, but that it can be eliminated. And so what his product really becomes, in essence, is assurance – not *in*surance, but *as*surance. D'you see? I've thought about it," he claimed, rotating his healed shoulder in a dominant gesture. "Life, let's say, is made up of atoms, little atoms, and each atom can be a worry to a person. And George, of course, thought about it and realized that we need to start at the smallest, indivisible level of granularity and deliver comfort there. Because isn't assurance a kind of certainty, and isn't certainty – in its way – a comfort?"

"I think it is," she said.

"Right," continued Caleb, assured. "He sifted the world, found that, and acted. It's admirable. That's foresight, and it will gnaw at your insides if you don't do something about it. But he did. Don't you think that's admirable?"

"I think it was," she said.

"Of course those atoms, those little worry-atoms, won't remain a cloud, diffuse and uncollected. There has to be some sort of confluence of resolved cares: the stuff's got to come together. Longshot flirts here with carbon, there with lithium, and hope that the nebula will remain in suspension. It must collapse, it *has* to, but will it be good for the company when it does?"

"I think it will be," she said.

"Good. I think so, too. He's got to have a plan. If only I knew what it was."

"But you don't know? I find that hard to believe."

Caleb started and the glove of his heart yawned wider. He looked across the table at her, at those platinum bangles and her caesium locks. She had his hand in her hand, cool and dry, hefting it. Each molecule of him bore down upon her palm, weighed and assayed, and she judged him.

"You are good, Caleb," she assessed. "You are what is needed."

8

Long ago, the first observation deck had been opulent, a sumptuous and dimly-lit expanse that ringed the Longshot Tower about a third of the way up the building's height. Furniture had been concentrated in nodes around its circumference, shaped for intimacy and professional confidence, under the pendulous clusters of lights. The view at that time was famous. Almost a century ago, the head of marketing had closed the deal of his life and then seduced that pneumatic specimen from the secretarial pool at the very same table, in the very same hour, gazing out over the slaughter-yards and the scented discharge plume from the paper mills. In the half-light, he'd toyed with those glamorous, amorous thighs and signed the fateful papers. "Tee hee!" she'd said. "Hoo hoo…" he'd said. Decades later the deck had been closed for want of interest. No one went there, so the view was shuttered and the elegant chairs and tables blanketed against the dust.

The space had been re-opened in recent years because breathing recirculated air had finally started to make everyone dizzy, after enough years. Consultants proposed unsealing the space and using it for mass gatherings *en plein air* – as a result the annual art show was instituted, but only after it had been demonstrated that that the simulated Festive Forest Retreat was really only making things worse. It was, naturally, a success. Every office from the division submitted its finest work from that year to the gallery for the appraisal and appreciation of any who chose to attend. There was also a panel that met separately and small prizes were awarded, usually mandatory time spent in the Executive Entertainment Center (EEC).

Caleb's team placed highly most years and so he considered taking Sophie with him to attend, really, as part of her onboarding process. There was so much to do. Of course he was dressed well: buttons, belts, brocades... if his work was on display, he knew that he would have to be as well. It was an imperative to showcase one's taste in clothing under such circumstances – almost a moral obligation – and he sought to meet it, even if doing so called for the heavy application of the synthetic scent he'd been hoarding. He arrived with the support staff to help with organizing things and to assist with the funneling of attendees into the exhibition. He was all smiles and ease and grace, and the fabrics flowed.

When Sophie arrived, he extended the palm and peeled back his very lips in welcome. She was perfect in frictionless velvet.

"It is good to see you," he said.

"It is good to see you," she replied. She took his arm and he steered her about and then towed her behind him to merge into the gallery traffic.

This year the gimmick was glasses. Each fibery canvas hung, seemingly blank, suspended from the inner wall that faced outward to the landscape beyond. But when viewed through the lenses provided by the event organizers, images suddenly became visible – the year's contenders. Caleb liked this sort of trick: it meant that the art was not accessible to all, but only to that great and noble few who, through the priestly intermediary of an optic, were permitted to behold the chosen works. It felt exclusive. It also prevented the art from intruding rudely and interfering with conversation, and so Caleb and Sophie were free to discuss the woman from the automotive department who'd killed herself last week. A narrow life she must have led and a repressed one, Sophie posited. Caleb nodded mature assent. They walked past advertisements for pet policies, dental policies, furniture, shipping, and malpractice policies. Everyone shuffled by in a slow, long line, circling the exhibit, glasses on and glasses off. There were little interfaces by each entry where one could sample the product, much as George had let Caleb sample one when he was in the infirmary. He tried to put in for something that would cover him for athlete's foot and was rather abruptly rejected. That seemed embarrassing. He tried not to let Sophie see.

Caleb made effort to focus on the crowd instead, after that. Despite all the recent winnowing occasioned by further automation, there was still quite the gathering. They all shifted slowly along, like solemn initiates; through his glasses, Caleb saw little halos refract around their bodies.

"Is this yours, Caleb?"

He settled his glasses on his nose again and focused. From the middle of the canvas, a figure surged. His toes, bloodied, pointed loosely downward to show he was suspended free of the ground, and with punctured hands he offered meat, cheese, and bread. From his shoulders branched twin golden arches, like wings, that peaked and fell to brace the holy land of Judea; the borders of that region were crowded in by a desolation and a confusion of discarded helms of every land and age and purpose, lost to dust. As a final detail, about his naked brow there spun a crown of concentric rings, dotted with fairy points, and a single, indivisible core shone in the middle of his forehead. "BUY MICROINSURANCE," it proclaimed across the top. And, beneath that, another line:

Now it is good and ever shall last –

Caleb felt immense pride, facing the piece: it

was a tasteless, semi-sensical pottage of distributed ideas, and it worked. Everything lay flat and dead on the surface of the canvas.

"Oh, Caleb," Sophie breathed. "This must be your work. It's so *like* you."

"Well…" stalled Caleb, his hands bashful in his pockets. It seemed appropriate to demur and pin the responsibility elsewhere, but it could not be denied: he was the Image Maker. Paternally, professionally he was deeply satisfied. Had he not perpetuated a moment of overwhelming magnificence? "I guess you could say I played my part, you know?"

"It's very pleasing."

It was time to reassert authority. "I hope you can see how much you have to learn here."

"Oh yes, yes, yes. Of course. It only makes sense that I would."

And it only made sense that she would. Just as it made sense for her to be there, with him, that evening. Last night he had checked again, as he had so many times before, for that elusive compatibility. He had plugged his details into his device along with hers just one more time and hoped that, for once, there might be hope… how pink the screen had gone! In a festival of light and noise, the necessity of their union had tolled out before him. It was a deliverance! Giddy, he had swum in the folds of his clothes and patted his fingertips together. His feet had kicked. Today, here, with her, he was self-assured and firm.

Knowing how the numbers lay, he gave himself over entirely to their authority as he discoursed; he vented little jets of language to tune the air as they walked, pointing and indicating, and she – naturally – had breathed it all in.

And he, naturally, had won. His piece was chosen; he was the victor. She applauded for him when the announcement came and he raised his arms as the congregation thundered his approval. Before him, the enthusiastic throng parted like a vapor, wisping away in recognition of his excellence and, in his tread, there was a resonance that sounded in the high places and sounded in the low. He approached the podium. The world seemed to shake with all the cheering he was hearing and the warm air blew in his face, through the lines cut in his hair with the faintest scent of bay as he advanced. With his first step onto the platform, a masculine energy pulsed through the whole assembly; the second raised a powerful reverberation that rattled the heart of each and all and caused the violent acclamation louder yet to grow. As he approached the apex, the whole chamber seized and sounded with his praise, most high.

He took the summit and he turned. The sound was deafening. He raised again his hands as if in benediction and gazed upon the crowd, towards the horizon. Victory flooded in his mind and, in a flash, he saw Vera, how he would dominate her, how he might drive her out. Yes, he saw her:

Buckle, fall, and be humble.

His teeth were grit and his eyes were hot and he knew how it would go, he knew it would be so. He opened his wide mouth to address the crowd and the rocking of his footfalls seemed to last somehow longer than they should. He focused again on the distant horizon, over the balcony. It was a fixed line out there, but the Longshot Tower seemed to be shaking. It was somewhat disconcerting. Troubling, really. Pictures started to drop off the walls and the podium slithered back and forth on the slick tiling. A feeble wailing arose in the confusion. Caleb struggled to stay upright, the maintenance of his dignity plummeting as a priority. Many of those present called out, buckled in fear, or covered their heads as plaster showered down from the ceiling in sheets. There was a sound, a horrible, guttural sound, as the innards and sinews of the architecture pulled against each other in a blind effort to remain whole. Everything cracked and everything swayed. Caleb saw, from his perilous, bucking perch, how few the people were that remained, how small they were, how vulnerable they seemed.

The tremors slowed and stopped; the building held its breath. Then the fire control system evacuated itself over the gathering, flooding the space with foam and fluid. Caleb descended the rostrum and approached the spot where Sophie cowered with her hands held over her face. He raised her up as the nozzles in the ceiling discharged their liquids upon them, liquids that ran in her hair, filled the seams in her skin, and pooled in his fashionable shoes. He took her hand and he led her away.

Caleb sloshed back to his apartment with Sophie, where they dried themselves and recomposed. He owned very little in the way of material things and his few possessions were mainly large appliances that were bolted in place, so his domicile was hardly disordered by the chaos that had shook the building. "An earthquake!" he breathed. When Sophie emerged from her toilet, he had already realigned everything and distributed himself across some furniture in a poised sort of comfort. On the table by his inclined shoulder he had rearranged the stuffed Longshot mascot he'd received when he finished the Microinsurance pilot project and a featureless, black object that Yoon had given him for some reason at a company function once. He'd heard that Yoon was trying to find a job and hadn't had much success as yet.

"Has there been any coverage yet?" Sophie asked and she tapped her cheeks and forehead dry.

"It's on just now," he said, and they watched. It had been a powerful, seismic event and the reporting showed its impact. Sophie gasped when she saw the concentric rings ripple across the map, pooling outward and ultimately zeroing back in on the epicenter, which was Longshot. Caleb excused himself for a moment, changed, and returned in brighter garments. The report continued: damage had been minimal, in spite of the terrifying magnitude of the event. There followed a sermon on the blessings of advanced earthquake-proofing technology and a demonstration of the planet's plates in their lazy movements, grinding away, one upon another. Sophie turned the display off; Caleb embraced her. They lodged that night, together, side by side.

Well before her, Caleb woke, and dressed while she was dreaming. Sophie, she was a beauty; so he lay his lips upon her cheek and kissed her drily as he left, hoping not to wake her. The hallways were plain and the elevators still in good working order. Everything smelled about the same, too, though it was puzzling that he would pay that much attention to his nostrils. Small things were amiss, he noted, in the aftermath of the quake: a misaligned wall hanging, a ceiling tile drifted out of place, exposing the unlit spaces above.

But the office was a disaster. Caleb entered the workspace to find its contents stirred into a terrifying chaos, and no thing left in that place where well it should be. Tables there were and lamps and chairs and lamps and tables... he could not count them. He walked into the middle of it, cutting through the waters of the waste, then he turned to look about himself.

"Oh, dear," he said, a-nibbling at his lip.

It was a wild overgrowth of wreckage. Mona's desk had toppled completely over and her worktop display had flown free of its anchor. All the doors gaped open and her unimportant, personal little somethings lay exposed amid the various refuse, part-hidden, like stones among the weeds. Two of the light fixtures were knocked out and the remainder were uncalibrated, so the room was lit in a somewhat green note. And pretty are the fallen things that lie before in ruin's shade, yes? He did not like it. And what was he to do to the place before the others showed? He assumed the cleaning services would be busy at this time with other rooms on other floors, and there would be no point even trying to summon them. But the girls needed to find him busy somehow, taking some sort of dynamic, executive action, when they arrived. He was certain of that. Caleb bent over, picked up a piece of office flotsam, positioned it on a proud little island in the sea of garbage, and then stepped back to look at the tiny order he had made. He felt sort of stupid for it.

But he kept at it, straightening this and lifting that, though he affected the layout of the whole but little. A half hour's effort had won him a small space an arm span in diameter that was clear of everything, down to the ground. But the room felt large, larger than ever. He moped. Disorder seemed to make everything bigger somehow and the refuse of the office lay about him in intimidating hectares. Turning about, he felt a kind of pathetic effort kindle in him, like a lighthouse on a barren rock trying to kindle the night with its single lamp. He checked the time; they would be here soon. Again, he found himself in a worthless kind of frenzy to effect change, much as he had been when he had labored to adjust his table and chair to convey to the ladies his new-minted authority, though that seemed long ago now.

He took up a piece of art that had fallen from its peg and held it in his hands. As he moved to lift it, he noted a curious puncture in the wall at about his eyes' height. It showed through to the room beyond.

"Hello, what's this?" he quizzed himself as he peered at the vacancy in space, but not really through it.

"Come look! Let me show you!" it seemed to beckon. The opening was minute, having perhaps the cross-section of a fresh young pea or the threading tendril of a plant.

"I don't know…"

"I invite and beckon!"

"Perhaps I shall?"

"But you must!" and he lay an eye to the rock-wall.

It was dark, within. Rather, after a moment, he

saw that it was dimly lit. The circumference of the hole was smooth and it had obviously been placed intentionally. He put a finger to its edge and punched slowly through, causing a faint shower of plaster – very fine – to descend. Beams of luminescence angled in to fall on gray forms and likenesses, almost visible but not quite articulate to the eye. He tightened his vision in upon itself and glanced about, hoping to detect something beyond.

"Here. I will help you," Mona said, approaching from behind. She lay her fingers wide upon the space beside the aperture, describing a lacquered pentacle with her broadly-spaced nails, and pushed. The plaster sundered and a ragged hole opened that showed more of the room adjoining. It was still quite dark. She edged Caleb out of the way and lay her bangled palms about the head-height wall-wound, and then she thrust. Great disks of brittle whiteness then branched and broke and came away in her hands as the opening widened, betraying more and more of what lay beyond. She tore away a sheet of the stuff that came off all in a piece – the size of a shield – and pulled it towards herself so they could both see in. Caleb looked.

It was just another dusty Longshot office, closed years ago when whoever was working there had been downsized and left. But there were footprints in the dust, he saw, showing on the blackened tile. Barefootsies. They went back and forth in a circuit, coming and going from the door to almost the place where Mona and he stood, and then once more to the door. Someone, it seemed, had been coming in here to gaze in upon them while they worked, through a peephole. Caleb felt strangely flattered, as if he were a tropical blossom caught in the photographer's lens just at the height of his bloom, when he was looking his best. He blushed a little, but tried to focus. All the old office's furnishings had been pushed into a far corner long ago and the quake had cast these into disorder, though they remained confined to their own side of the room. On the wall was written:

You gambol near, seek cover from the rain.
His eyes are mad. His breath is warm.
He parts your skin and reaches in.
You give – the sapling in the storm,
The gasping votive to His sin.

They were such nice colors, weren't they? Such very varied colors. They always are... and the meter is good for Caleb, too, the way the poem walks, its cadence. His thought is interrupted; he sees the trusting lamb in white, the reddened hand that moves and moves, and the agate sky above, all written out in green and blue and yellow. And the storm is not yet a fury, but very insistent, and you know the future when you see it, the clouds and the coiling thunderheads. It is so warm in a rainy summer…

Beside him, Mona made a terrible noise in her nostrils and drove the blank of plaster into the ground with a crack. She pushed it down and kept pushing until both her narrow arms had straightened and locked at the elbow. Colorless shards flew and powder rose as she exerted herself. Then it was silent.

"Oh!" she heaved. "I cannot *believe* this!"

"What is it?" Caleb asks, lost for one final moment.

"This is horrible. Something must be done. Don't you agree?"

"I do," Sophie assented.

Caleb repositioned himself so that he could see both of them. He had not heard Sophie come in. Just now and for the first time he noticed that she and Mona were the same height and also – since Sophie's transformation – similarly proportioned. Standing side by side, their collarbones, lips, eyebrows, chins, and hairlines were all on a level with each other, like the lines in a sheet of music. They spoke to him:

"Look at this mess!"

"A sty!"

"Look at it!"

"Obscene!"

"Inappropriate!"

"How *could* she?"

"It had to be her!"

"Who else?"

"Who indeed!"

"Obscene!"

Caleb's eyes played ping-pong. The two of them talked and gestured and talked and he felt himself fade from the interaction, brushed aside. When the twins and the cousin arrived, the conversation rose to a new and spiny intensity; it was a great, heated foment of disbelief. How could she? He didn't quite understand what was going on and he didn't appreciate being let slide, which seemed to be happening. Caleb could feel it: they were all objects in motion around a central point, which was Purpose, and his centrifugal force alone was too strong to keep him in orbit. Unmoored, he spun away from the group and came to rest in the space where his workstation had been. There he found the desk clock he'd stacked on the over-turned file server again, staring at him. He felt stupid all over again.

But then he righted his desk and he righted his chair and he stared at them while they chattered. They were like a porcupine of pointing that made noise, he thought. He hauled his tabletop console and the peripherals out of the sea of drifting waste and tried powering them up to see if they still worked. They did, and it was something of a relief to see that it was so.

From the outset, it was clear that whatever they were intending to do would be a lengthy undertaking. After furious debate, they approached his altar in a line abreast and declared their desire to rehabilitate the adjoining room, by hand if need be. He raised his palm in benediction and bid them to it. In a way, to him, it seemed strange, it really did, how powerful, how united and decisive their reaction was; he also assumed that it had been Vera there, the one who'd owned the room, the one who'd changed it. Further, he remembered these self-same ladies charging him into the closet, where he assumed that Vera's many-colored writings must have been an influence as well... What had changed? Something had changed, he knew it. How could these quondam partisans of an agitator unseen turn – with such vehemence and conviction – back again upon their erstwhile hegemon? He was impressed with himself for being able to pose such a question, but knew not the answer; it was simply obvious that it was so.

A more pressing question was what he intended to do with himself while they scrambled about. As he gave his approval for their enterprise, they exploded in all directions and then drained out the front door of the office. Soon after they returned with mops, dust pans, carts and every other thing imaginable; he nodded to each one as she returned, never moving from his desk. But it was obvious that he could not do this forever and appear to remain relevant. What to do?

This is when he remembered the investigation.

Or the purge, or whatever it was. Vera. The thing with Vera. Getting rid of her. It occurred to him that he'd never bothered to learn about exactly what the nature of her claim had been. If she had a claim to collect, then there must have been a policy that was broken, he reasoned, and it was his responsibility as an investigator to uncover the details. This resolution filled him with a Purpose of his own.

Caleb focused on this new task and then gave himself to it. The company file system was large, but he knew its organization in a very deep way so finding the files he needed was no major task.

Nevertheless, there was so much. Vera's file was a mountain of unsorted ore, stripped from an impure vein, and dumped in a heap that towered high, to touch the sky… It was a huge repository of information, completely uncatalogued; browsing through the mass of it, Caleb found that he was uncertain how even to determine the nature of her claim. He probed the files, looking at the names – he found nothing specifically from Longshot, but it was obvious that she had held many, many jobs before at many different places, though none of them seemingly for long. It occurred to him, in an underwhelmed and sinking sort of way, that the difficulty he was facing in finding her insurance information might be partially by design. Could someone have decided that it aligned with the Founder's intent to hide vital documentation in a field of sameness, like a gem in a starry sky, where it might not easily be found? It sounded possible. Caleb was bold and opened something at random.

It was a video file. An image of Vera appeared, seated in a chair, against a pallid background. The camera caught her at a three-quarter perspective, as she engaged in dialogue with someone off screen. She looked much younger.

He heard a man's voice, one reading from a prepared document. He sounded old, a grandfather, and he spoke a weary, drawn-out manner. He must have been seated close to the recorder and the tired texture of his language and his breathing was pronounced.

"Are you aware of the magnitude of what you have done, the pain you have caused, great as your own may have been?" Caleb could hear his lips touch when he spoke. "If you persist in this state, it won't look good for you, and things aren't going well already."

The video quality was poor and Caleb could see little detail in her face, though it was obviously Vera. Under the wild of her hair, she had a bull's forehead – very broad – and her eyes were angularly shaped, with a bovine turn to them. She wore a sloppy-looking custodial uniform, but of a different company. Her response was indistinct.

"Can you hear me and can you clearly respond?"

"I forgot what I had said just now."

"Into whose home did you go after the wedding?" he queried.

She made a response. Caleb's couldn't hear it over the questioner's breathing. Not that it would have mattered, without context. Someone got married sometime in the past and she was there for it. Had there been cake? He assumed.

"And what child was born in the house to – " then the footage terminated. Whatever followed had not been preserved.

There was a write-up appended; Caleb found that it was not a transcript, which he had expected, but a synopsis of the events leading up to the inquiry by the unknown figure. There had been an incidence of workplace violence. Vera, he read, had incited a young manager's mother to physically attack her son. An additional note stated that the man's sisters and his wife had also taken part in the assault. Caleb found a picture of the poor employee's head and he was startled at how terribly lacerated his face had been.

The women scrubbed and pulled and hauled their things about; Caleb sat and browsed for the rest of the day. As they carried broken furniture past, he stared at a series of shipping manifests and a couple of scans of pilot IDs, all with different names, but the exact same picture. For the life of him, he could see no connection between any of the items in the dossier; most of them didn't even contain an obvious reference to Vera. By the time they had returned, having disposed of a therapeutic massage chair and two standing desks, he was pondering a trove of photographs, all taken of plastic fruit in various settings – the beach, a funeral parlor, the hair dresser's... He stared at these various artifacts and others until the day ended. Sophie went home with him to another meticulous meal, where they dined across the table from each other, to the piped-in accompaniment of harp music and choral tunes.

Sophie went back to her cleaning the following morning and Caleb returned to his documents. After three days, she and the other girls had cleared the space out, scrubbed and polished the surfaces that needed it, and brought in new fixtures. They invited him in to make an inspection and he was impressed by how terribly clean the floor was. Caleb reviewed their work and told them that he was pleased – perhaps they all deserved little stuffed animals? He went back to his work station and felt intimidated by the mass of Vera's file and small – quite small – before the eminent wealth of it.

9

Caleb developed a horrifying case of athlete's foot. It had started as the tiniest artist's touch of pink around the base of his toes the day after he'd been showered on in the award ceremony, and by the time he finished his tour of the room, it had exploded into full, feverish florets, with little crusty auras that touched his toenails. He hobbled. As a matter of pride, he determined not to show it, but when the caustic itchies grabbed him and he staggered, he tried to let it happen with a vanquished majesty, like a wounded king about to topple. There were times when he could hardly contain the dancing of his troubled feet beneath the desk, as he watched the team at work. Ultimately, he caved and sought a remedy.

The tube was immaculate and bright. He squeezed a pretty curl of the cure from its end and rubbed the stuff straight in, lacing his fingers deep between his lower digits. O, the quenching immediacy of relief! O, the calming of the nerves, the taming of their torrid, liquid rage... O, the rapture and the transport at the banishment of pain, the sunshine coming at storm's end! By the very next day he considered himself healed, whole again. Fresh, really. Better almost than after his stay at the clinic, after that she-beast had bit him.

Sophie even toyed with his feet now, every once and again. She held them in her finished fingertips.

Later on, considering the ladies' annual performance reviews, Caleb tried to put the image of Sophie's slick little grippers, gliding between his toes, very far from his mind. Very, very far. He tried to put the humming noise she emitted when she did this quite out of his mind as well. He was making an exceptional effort, in fact. He focused on the forms. Someone was going to get a bonus – but who? There wasn't much to go on: in the interest of keeping things fair and preventing bias, all personal details had been stripped and replaced with blanks or strings of numbers. The information the girls had been permitted to provide was also, itself, largely numeric and mapped along various scales, which could be plotted on a graph if you pressed a button. Caleb did this and then squinted at the resulting buckshot distribution, spread across three axes, trying to puzzle out who each applicant was. Impossible. He compared one with the next and found that the differences between the two were significant without being important, if that made any sense. Maybe it did? The ladies had been allowed to write brief opening statements, so he directed his attention towards these. The first one ran:

I was the sign of bright day.

The second:

My works all shined forth through the cloud.

He manipulated documents within the viewing frame so that he could see the last two together:

I was a golden line of bright light.
I burned signs across ages.

Caleb confessed himself lost at this point. Craning around his display, he reconnoitered the females: they sat there with their backs to him, pumping out product. Mona, Sophie, the cousins, and the twins all glided up and down as they worked, bouncing in their seats like feminine pistons, synchronized to the slow-stroke of industry, in-taking, compressing, igniting, and expelling images, all for the advancement of the enterprise. It was wonderful to behold; they didn't seem to need him.

"And am I really so unnecessary?" Caleb asked himself. "Have I become the unwanted overflow? Effluvium? That dry froth of old waste that is scraped off the top and slung away?" It seemed not to be so; he suspected he would have been eliminated by this point if he was.

But Caleb's apparent redundancy worried him. Shaking it off, he busied himself for a while trying to determine if any one of the applicants was, in fact, demonstrably more qualified than the others, but this proved just as difficult as attempting to figure out who was who. Assuming, as he did, that upward trends were meritorious, everyone's level of achievement appeared to be identical on the whole. There was one packet whose data appeared, on one graph, to trace a line that looked something like a seagull or a tern. That could be good! Caleb liked birds. He was psyching himself up for choosing this person, whoever she was, when the door opened and a technician appeared.

"I have a work order," he announced, approaching Caleb's station. "I'm here to put in the new fire control system."

"Let's see it then," said Caleb, declining to rise. He didn't lean forward at all either, so the man was obliged to reach across the whole expanse of Caleb's desk to pass him the device containing the permit. Turning it about, he saw that the tech had been sent to install a brand new gaseous flame suppressor within such and such a time frame. With a snappy sort of twirl he returned the thing and bid the man to go about his business.

Letting the performance appraisals slide for a moment, Caleb mused over the worker as he did his job, coolly assessing the situation. If the old sprinklers were out, there had to be a reason of some sort… Property damage, he concluded, was the motivation behind the new system's installation. When the sprinklers had needlessly activated at the art show, everything had been soaked, including many things that were probably never intended to be wet: not only the art in the gallery, but the upholstery, too, and the carpeting, and any of the exposed computer systems, etc. Almost all of it would need to be replaced. It came down to a question of costs. Caleb nodded as the slick logic of moving to a gas-based delivery system became apparent to him, but he found it fearful. He inquired of the tech what sort of medium would be used to quench the flames. An aerosol, perhaps? No. Argon. It would be argon. He did not think that he, Caleb, could probably breathe argon. Sophie didn't look like she could either. In his mind there flashed the image of the two of them, her in his arms, flames dwindling in the background, and Sophie gasping hopelessly at him as she struggled to draw air. Her tortured, piteous image loomed before him! He felt the impulse to contract in his chair, fought it, overcompensated, and pitched forward, slamming into the desktop with a flat noise like a deer hitting a windshield.

"Ow," he said, putting his hand to his nose. It seemed alright. No one in the room appeared interested in his sudden faceplant; they were all too absorbed in their work. He recovered his composure. Turning to his workstation, he found that the pension fund that owned his pituitary gland had already written him a strongly worded letter, reminding him of his responsibilities as custodian of their assets.

Caleb worried over the annual review for the rest of the day, molested by unwelcome images conjured from his brain – scenes of paralysis and asphyxiation. Throughout this, the technician was chatty. As he fitted pipes and pumps together, he discoursed to the unresponsive room about the merits of the system he was installing, its numerous advantages over conventional fire-control solutions, its efficiencies, etc. He talked also about the strange things he'd found in the tower as he'd serviced its various departments: things left behind, things lost, things embarrassing to their owners, things inexplicable… At one point, he'd even had to cut the lock off a door that someone had chained shut in the strangest way. Now why would someone do a thing like that? There had been a right mess inside, too, and no denying it. Caleb muttered, puttered back and forth, trying to decide if he should go for the woman with gull-shaped data, or the other one that was more suggestive of a tuffet. In the end, he went with his initial impulse and chose the bird lady. The technician finished his job, cleaned up, and then everyone went home.

Caleb slept terribly that night, partly from the cold, because he refused to lie under the covers;

he had a morbid fear that his bedsheets would find their way into his mouth, down his windpipe, into his lungs, and suffocate him. Argon! The cooling system was on full-blast, blowing a dry, melancholy air across his body, so that he had to curl himself up tight as a fist for warmth. In the end, he slept. He dreamed. Caleb dreamed strange dreams. He saw:

> About the tender body rise
> Such trees as flower to the skies,
> That shadows scatter. O, young leaf –
> Who to the flock provides relief –
>> Wither now! *You* cook his veins,
>> Sear him white 'til ash remains.
>> Dominate! You are the *Sun*.
>> Bake the hills! Where rivers run
>>> Vapor only carries now.
>> Boil the cloud! Prevent the rains!
>>> Drive the sunbeam as the plow!
>> Green recedes; bright stone now gains…
>>> Devastate and cauterize –
>>> Blast the plain that 'round him lies.

> Gold-shining in your light, the cities mount,
> All full of spires, full of men who count.
>> About Him now your flames advance and grow
>>> Pain lines His brow
>>> Who, shifting now,
>>> Did turn and run, turn and run,
>> Turn and run and, turning, show
> That though He sought to flee th' advancing Sun,
> Your holocaust consumes the world as One.

He tossed and turned. He woke; he lay prone, blinking in the darkness. This would not do. Anxiety squirmed about under his skin, between the fat and muscle, and it denied him rest. He got up and whispered little things to himself as he pulled a robe on. Caleb was drawing on his silly-looking slippers as he tried to think of a place to go for a walk, to perambulate, when he remembered the tech's comment about cutting a lock off a door somewhere. It was possible, he supposed, that it was the very door he'd chained shut shortly after Vera's arrival, to keep her out. It would be as good a place to go as any… he set off.

The lock was gone, struck away. He pushed open the door and found that the room beyond had been tidied up and given a good scrub. It had become as clean as the chamber next to his own office. Caleb stepped inside and did a little turn, his cozy rabbit feet guiding him forward and about. Equipment in the room hummed merrily, all lit up, and a bust of the Founder in his snakeskin raiment was visible beside a console, on a tabletop that was otherwise bare. Not a shred of the reams of paper that Yoon had once dumped so regularly down the ventilation shaft remained. Caleb left the room and shuffled about the building for another hour or so, looking into various chambers; the new fire control system had been installed in most of them. He cringed back to bed and got what rest he could.

Caleb was blinking with fatigue the next day

when the winner received her award. The gull-lady turned out to be one of the twins – the one on the left? – and she was enjoying her prize.

"Thank you! Thank you all!" she exhaled, gripping the mandatory stuffed animal, a bipedal goat with googly eyes. "I couldn't have done it without you!" The Longshot logo flashed between her fingers.

Mona and Sophie applauded grimly. They and the other twin had all received consolation prizes of a free trial of Microinsurance. That evening, Sophie had given her policy to Caleb to do with as he chose. It was one of those "sample" packages that could be defined by the user and then accepted or rejected by the company, as seen fit. For free!

"Argon suffocation," he boldly supplied, after an anxious eternity of struggle. For the period of validity he put "1,000 yrs." A millennium.

The screen turned pink. He was insured! When news came the next day that there was a training scheduled for the new system and a drill to follow, he was pleased to hear it. He was going to be the fire warden! Even in an emergency, he noted, they were still relying on him to be The Manager. Thus was he doubly relieved.

"Come now!" he called to everyone, rapping the table surface as he read to the ladies aloud from the announcement, proclaiming the training and the drill. Doubtlessly they had received it as well, but he was feeling cheerful today and in a mood to be dominant. "Hear! Hear! There's important goings-on today. We are to report to the Learning Center! Your times and seat assignments have been disseminated to you. Please, all of you, don't forget to check your mail!"

The ladies all turned back to their work stations. He had interrupted them in the middle of doing just the thing he'd tasked them with, so they simply got back to their business. Caleb consulted his own message and found that he was not due to receive his own training until close to the end of the day. That was fine. The Learning Center was large, but had never been intended to provide company-wide Education Experiences to everyone all at once. Such classes were, accordingly, staggered across the day in repeated sessions and the employees were serviced in batches. Caleb felt quite excited about his coming Education Experience, so much so that his obvious irrelevance to the operation of the office ceased to bother him. The hours stretched on, seemingly endlessly, and to no particular end – it troubled him not. Even if he did no real work, he told himself, at least he was presiding. His role was a ritual one, in a way. When it came close to time for him to leave, he snuck out early to avoid the potential awkwardness of having to go somewhere with someone.

Domed in white the cavern was, and edged around in stone. He'd been to the Learning Center many times before, usually for award ceremonies or annual reports on the health of the company, when the news was good. Caleb wasn't quite certain what the contours of the ceiling were, but he assumed it was a vaulted lozenge shape: the lighting was always so bright up there, against the featureless surface of it, that staring straight up was like gazing into a vapor. It was simply a blank, and illumination was cast down upon the rows and rows of unfilled seats from above. He walked an arbitrary distance forward and perched himself somewhere, one or two spaces in. He knew it wasn't quite the spot he was supposed to be in, but he was close to it. For whatever reason, the algorithm that assigned seating had not cottoned on to the fact that company staffing had been reduced drastically in size, and so it still reserved room for all the terminated employees. This meant that the few people who still showed up for these events were always scattered far and wide about the auditorium. He scanned the periphery and saw a person here, a person there, settling in, all of them quite distant. Caleb leaned back in his chair and stared up at the ceiling again.

It was so white; it was limitlessly white. Looking up into it, he could sense no distance and he felt no field of focus. The limits of his vision blurred. His eyes burned. The room was quiet, so quiet that he could hear nothing, and in the clean, clean room there was nothing to be smelled either, no scent. All he could feel was the gravity, hanging from his clothes. He felt something happen inside his skull and his lips were moving silently. There were shapes, up there. Faces. Caleb had hazy impressions of human simulacra coming at him, faintly, from behind a wall of smoke. He saw the darknesses of their eyes and lips stiffen to be pronounced and then submerge again, never having become properly individual. They came and went and he watched them as they came and went, and then he recognized Mona. It was her, but only for a second. He saw a twin next. Their faces boiled out of the void, were visible to him for a moment, and then vanished. He saw George – and he saw George again. Sophie came at him next, projecting forcefully downward at him from the apex to hold in crisp resolution, just long enough for him to see the careful contour of an eyebrow. The twins – both of them, this time. The faces came in pairs now, and in threes, turning and moving as an orchestrated line. They were a circle. They were so clean. Caleb felt at ease. In the midst of them all, the Founder emerged, grew large, and opened wide his mouth. He spoke.

> We will not stand in the shade;
> Our force will command, overpower.

The words showered down on Caleb; they were as sunshine and brass. He lay way far back with his mouth wide open and his eyes dilated into the emptiness, experiencing. On all sides, the room had become unimportant or simply ceased to exist. The silence around him was a bell and the bell was perfect. He was transported.

And sneaking up behind him, on tired, colored, footsteps, came a voice. The tones were faded now, but Caleb listened. He smelled smoke and his nostrils twitched. Then he moaned. Caleb adjusted himself a little, and someone spoke to him.

"You're in my chair, Caleb."

It was Mona.

"You don't sit here. You sit over *there*." He looked at her and she pointed.

"Did you say something just now?"

"I said 'You're in my chair, Caleb.'"

"No. Not that. Something about a man on fire?"

"What?"

And he quoted to her from his memory:

> *About Him now your flames advance and grow*
> *Pain lines His brow*
> *Who, shifting now,*
> *Did turn and run, turn and run,*
> *Turn and run and, turning, show*
> *That though He sought to flee th' advancing Sun,*
> *Your holocaust consumes the world as One.*

"No." She made a lemon face. "Who would ever say a thing like that? Now scoot over."

"Where?"

"You don't know your own seat? There." She pointed to a spot, two spaces over. "Move, will you? Please? It's not like it's my choice. Or yours either, actually."

Dutifully, Caleb rose and replaced himself with two empty chairs between him and Mona. He always sat here and she always sat there; Kelly and Sally used to sit between them, but they had been let go a long time ago. In the theater, somewhere, Yoon probably still had a spot reserved with his name on it.

"Thank you. I really prefer to keep things clean like this."

They sat, apart from each other. It took but a moment for Caleb to descend into agonies: having employed guile to avoid the potential awkwardness of having to go somewhere with someone, he now found himself going *nowhere* with a subordinate. He almost opened his mouth to speak, but realized there was nothing he could say. Caleb wished to communicate familiarity, easy authority, the austere superiority of command, and a solicitous simper all at once, in a single sentence, and simply failed. His entrails were winding up inside him like a clock, coiling around a central, twisting key. He felt his pores dilated cavernously in the anticipation of a drenching, drowning sweat, but his body was a husk, desiccated to its core, and there was no wellspring on which to draw. His skin twitched as it did something like heaving. He did not feel good.

"Can you stop making that noise?"

"I'm not making any noise."

"It's a sort of high-pitched, squeaky sound."

"I'm not making any noise."

"Whatever." Mona had been looking at him as she spoke, but now she turned away to pay attention to something on her far side for a moment. She worried at whatever it was until it either came free or was fixed, which seemed to satisfy her. "Have you heard the latest about that Vera woman yet?" She turned back to face him.

"No, I've not," he confessed. "Tell me about it." Giving her a command helped him recover a little. He started to find the space between them comforting as well.

"Well, it's weird. I don't like it. She was apparently cleaning up some room somewhere – or, at least, pretending to – in the animal policies section. The floor below it. You know, the place where they do the cats and dogs and racehorses and all that? So, she's down there, with her mop, and she's taking way too long to finish, so the boss sends someone to check in on her."

Caleb knew the office and thought he might know who this person might be. "It wasn't…?" he asked, and gestured to a particular feature on his face. He felt embarrassed to verbally identify anyone by so obvious an imperfection in so prominent a spot.

"Yes!" Mona seemed happy he'd hit on it. "Her! Anyway, she went on down to check on her, and the floor was just *slick* when she entered. It must have been some sort of utility room or something, I think; otherwise it would have been carpeted."

"Or it could have been one of the old server closets," Caleb offered, "from back before they consolidated all the computing in the sub-basements."

"Also possible. Either way, there was standing water on the floor when she got there and Vera's just sitting in the middle of it, with her stupid bucket turned upside down between her knees, and she's tapping on the bottom of it."

"With what? Her hand?"

"How should I know? Probably. I don't know. But she was tapping."

"Then what?" Caleb asked. "Tell me what happened next."

"She – the woman who went down there, y'know – she approached Vera, walked up to her, to see if something's the matter or whatever, and Vera lunges at her!"

"Lunges?"

"Lunges! Can you believe it? Grabs her around the waist!"

The lights began to dim; the Learning Experience was about to start. Mona tried to continue talking, but Caleb shushed her with a bold command. The room darkened completely, to an abyssal pitch, and Caleb was alone again. The screen at the very front of the chamber lightened and content began to display. It was one of those presentations done in universal symbols, mostly ungendered humanoids caught stomping through the act of the coming fire drill, in its various stages.

"So she lunges, and…," Mona continued, from the vacant darkness.

"Sssht!" Caleb insisted, ordering the vacuum to obey. He was watching now a demonstration of what *not* to do in the event of a fire drill – or an actual fire – at the Longshot HQ, which involved jumping out of highly-placed windows. Before his eyes, little stick figures made poor decisions and gambled foolishly with their lives. The presentation was punctuated with a kind of audio that was emphatically not music, but still added something to the epideictic nature of it all. The ill-considered suicides' impacts, for example, were marked with a discordant twanging noise.

Caleb focused: the first section appeared to treat the duties and equipage of the fire warden, and therefore concerned him directly. He was surprised to find that he was not to lead everyone in his charge to a place of common refuge. This was counter to his expectation, which had been that he would guide his ragged flock to some tranquil place, where he would look over them and be a bulwark against the inferno beyond, perhaps working in close coordination with a distant, central command, orchestrating all. Instead, he learned that he was to exercise his unique privileges as a guarantor of safety to secure his charges in pre-assigned cells, each one isolated from the other. He was further surprised to discover that they were, once penned in, to apply a breathing apparatus on penalty of suffering a grisly set of animations, indicative of slow death. From this, he concluded that the drill would be a live-fire exercise. Live fire? He chuckled to himself. It meant, he corrected, that real argon would be used. The final instruction was that he was to brandish a rod of authority and clear his sector one story at a time, sealing each floor as he moved upward towards that next. None of it looked particularly difficult. Caleb relaxed; he put his hands behind his head and slouched in his chair. It would be easy.

"You were saying?" he asked the darkness.

Mona did not immediately respond. He waited. He did not know how long he waited; there was no way to tell, really. Images whisked by onscreen and he looked at them, assuming that Mona was simply focusing on something of interest to her. Sooner or later, she would respond.

"Oh yes," she said. "I said she lunges, right?"

"You did."

"Well, there's not much to share after that. She grabs at what's-her-face, and… then, I mean, the lady bolted. She bolted and filed a complaint, actually. And, by the time the investigation got underway, that Vera person was gone. No one's really sure where? I heard that her closet was full of those stuffed animals they hand out, but they were, like, shredded."

"I don't like that."

"I don't like it either. Her room's been sealed, but I don't see what else could be done."

"Was there anything else? Any other details?"

"That's it, I think. It's awful. Let's focus on our Learning now."

Caleb stared at the Learning. It was pretty valuable, he decided. He knew that Mona – over there, wherever she was – felt the same way that he did. He felt a little lonely watching it, but he was fine, really.

Learning was good because it was improving, and the accumulated store of Caleb's own Learning was vast, by this point, but there was always a very great deal more out there for him to acquire. His mind was like a landscape of bins and boxes, mouths open to the downpour of information, broadcast from above. It wasn't really important to him that he know everything about everything that was in all of them, but it mattered greatly that he know where to find what he needed. When a question came or decision-making called, there was usually something out there that was solidly right, and he needed to be right… across the pitted meadow of his mind, little facts showered and were sown like stones. He was aware of the landing of each of them, and of its final resting place. He was not tired. He kept on watching, watching… the disjointed soundtrack of the video started to bleed together and became like a choir of harps playing in unison, harmonious to his ear. For the drill to come off properly, there were many things that he would need to know and do, as Warden, or the risks would be intense. He studied them all.

After the Learning, he walked straight back to Sophie, avoiding everyone else along the way. He didn't even bother to look where Mona went.

10

On the morning of the actual drill, Caleb talcumed up his skinny limbs and slid his trousers on. He'd had his whole suit retailored and finally – having been too tight before and then loose all over, after his stay in the clinic – the fit was perfect. His silhouette whispered of divinity. Caleb shaved his cheeks and chin to a baby pink, fashioned his hair, and applied light fragrance to complete the human image. Such a fashionable likeness! So pure and perfect: gold all over and forever young!

"Sophie, here," he said to her. "Help me on with these."

In the sanctum of his apartments, the acolyte assisted him. From the table's surface, Sophie raised his Warden's sigil. The badge of his new office was a sliver plaque of taut wire, showing the title of his rank in the middle, surrounded by a blowing wreath; she slotted the tab at the back into his breast pocket and let it slide to anchor. He raised his arms, like wings. She roped the girdle around him and cinched it fast. At this, Caleb purred relief: if he had not had his pants taken in, there was no way it would have fit over the cloth, about his waistline, without unseemly bunchings. In his heart he knew that such fair coincidences occurred not at random, but were ever the auguries of success foretold. He took up the staff and then laid it aside, within arm's reach of his chair.

"Leave me. Go to the office," he bid her. Sophie gathered up her things and departed, leaving him unattended in the room. Caleb stood before the mirror and observed himself. Everything pleased him. The belt clung to the zone above his hips in martial firmness, dappled with life-saving accessories and communicators. His badge twinkled, glowed. But it was the staff that would complete the picture... he caught it up again and held it before him in the manner of a javelin at rest, with the center of gravity lain upon his slightly upturned forearm. The sensors at either end of the rod pulsed with energy. Perfect. Absolutely perfect. Perfectly perfect? No... just, perfect. In pleasure, his heart squirmed.

There was, however, no time for such indulgences now: Caleb had work to do. As Warden, he needed not only to oversee the safe evacuation of everyone within his quadrant of the building – the whole tower – but he was, moreover, responsible for ensuring that all the residual gases were safely purged after the exercise, and, before all else, that everything was properly in place at the start. This final task, first in the process, was essential, and he left now to accomplish it, his accouterments a-sway with every step.

Caleb began with the hallway just outside his apartment, checking the displays beside every door to confirm that pressure levels were properly equalized and everything topped up with sufficient power. He was meticulous in this... to be honest, he was dawdling. The structure of his duties felt unbalanced to him, because he only had to visit the rooms right now that would be inhabited during the drill, which were few, but afterwards he was required to patrol every floor, all the way down to the basement, to observe the safe conclusion of the exercise; such bald asymmetry held an ugly flavor for him, and he would not make himself rush to meet it. He took slow steps, almost as if he were wading through oil, mineral essences up to his waist, deep in thick lubricants. For his neighbor he made a healthy triple-check of everything before nosing along, lingering over every index unnecessarily. His thoughts on why he chose to operate in such a manner were not articulate, but an impulse told him that he was, in some way, laying his thumb to the scales and forcing an equilibrium. And equilibrium was just.

Three levels below he came to the floor where he knew the twins lived. He had never been in their room; he strained to look in at the portal with his nose almost to the glass, trying to see what one might see in there. It was dark. Caleb actually saw more of his own face reflected back at him than he saw of the world inside. There was nothing to be heard from within either. He began to worry that he might have misidentified the apartment and that this would actually be someone else's room; that would make him wrong, and he did not want to be wrong. What if the room was empty, unoccupied for potentially years after the elimination of some then-redundant department, left sere and fallow? He lowered his head and marched onward, worriedly huffing off under a cloud. He was miffed at himself, but scared in a small way as well: the emptiness of Longshot Tower felt apparent to him. It was a honeycomb of vacant cavities, and he stalked among them on his mission, fundamentally alone. He grew scared. He picked up his pace. Inadvertently, he rushed through much of the remainder of his watch and finished much earlier than he had intended. The demands of balance then obliged him to retrace his path and visit once again the corridors he had just left, but this time with an intentional, insulating inattention: he simply confirmed for a final time that every cell was ready and gave no heed to the identity of any particular occupant. At the end of his long line and many levels up from where he had restarted his inspection, he came upon a door, with something stuck upon it. Paper? It reminded him of Yoon. No longer quite certain where he was, among the halls, he took the folded sheet down and laid it open. The writing inside was all colored in pinks and blues and greens…

Vera?

He stifled something in his throat and made his hands refold her verse to put into his pocket. Was she still here? And where was he? He looked around, but the hallway seemed the same as any other. Consulting the room number, he found himself outside his own unit. Preposterous! In his breast a nozzle opened an issued an austere, purifying fire that jetted within him as a hissing column, and his ears grew hot as irons. What to do? He did not know what he might do. As Caleb stood half-meditating in his vengeful mode, his timer went off and he saw that he was due back at the office for the start of the exercise. He regained focus. It was good to be reminded of something.

By the time he had come to the office, the warning lights were going, cautioning everyone to prepare. The girls all rose as he entered; he spoke to them briefly. It was all very easy. And, as he talked, the violet lamp high up in the corner agitated from above, intermitting on and off. His audience changed: it was the people before him, then it became haloed, lilac outlines that just showed the suggestion of identity, then it was women again, then another set of standing figures. As long as he focused on himself and the fact that he was talking, the words came. He was giving instructions. When he had finished all that he meant to tell them, they filed out of the room like objects down a chute somewhere and went to their separate refuges. Caleb was then alone again, hung with the regalia of his office, in the sometimes purple room.

Anxiety rapidly crowded back upon him; he remembered the vacant halls below and they troubled him. He had also given his monitory address too quickly and dismissed the girls before he really meant to, leaving himself again with heavy, useless, unbalancing minutes before the signal came to start. He began to think of argon again, and how scary it was. Caleb was alone, all by himself. Argon would kill him – it would come from behind, from below and kill him. He knew that it wouldn't, but it might anyway. His nerves wrothe up and down his body and commanded him to do something. Inadvertently opening his hands, he let the staff with all the precious doodads in it drop with a clatter, and that startled him. He picked it up and leaned it against a table, where it would be safe. Now, Caleb felt horribly threatened; anything in the room might shift or rattle at any moment. His hands wanted to do something again, so he punched them deep in his pockets – a tight fit – trying to suffocate their energy. Instead, he found Vera's paper. He drew it out and gave it a look:

His feet but dot the frying sands
As faster yet – and faster yet – his hands
Scythe through the with'ring grasses. See
How his divine, unhinged velocity
   Far, *far* Him drives in rout.
    His smoke's in the air,
    Your flame's in his hair,
   As – panicked – his wind gives out.
Revenge, revenge pours from the skies;
  Iron columns arise!
  Molten beams down You cast,
  Sterilizing in your blast

 All the pastures, as your rays incise
  Deep in the land. Advance!
  Stop his song! End the dance!
Drive Him from the earth, then crucible the seas –
    And heed you not his pleas –
    But run Him to his knees;
   With his final moans,
   Burn Him in his bones.

Behold Him now trudge the surf-foam: He fears
   As the vapors rise under your gaze
And scald into air at your masculine blaze.
The seabed's lain bare and the moment, it nears:
At his quivering heart then You angle your spears
    And kindle his frame
    To make coals of his fame
And a coke of his limbs and an ash of his years.

Reading the lines, Caleb felt significantly worse. He felt like sick garbage. If the argon didn't kill him, the building was sure to actually catch fire somehow and he'd be crisped right where he stood. He just knew it. He was, in fact, positively certain. Come to think of it, his chances of survival would probably be greater if he relocated to the hallway, even though it wasn't what doctrine called for. He started towards the door, purposely, but then images from the Learning began occurring to him: all those poor stick figures… If he went out into the hallway, in advance of his cue-time, his limbs would probably be horribly divided from his body one way or another, or he'd find a way to trip and fall from a terrible height, ending his life as an abstract streak on the pavement. Anxiety drew him towards the door, but fear repelled him from it, too. He stood, held in half-stride, caught in a terrible agony of suspense, drawn taut. The tone of the light in the room shifted down half a step and to an urgent indigo, still throbbing, which he recognized as a sign that initiation was imminent. It would be go-time, then. He was still strung up midway through his uncompleted stride, but his hackles rose and his knuckles cracked and his eyes did roll and his pupils gaped.

Then it was blue; it collapsed into blue. Cerulean. Blue, ocean blue. Steady. Ocean blue: get out of the water. Blue. Go-blue. Make for the green hallway, green is land. Go. Learning activated; he was in motion. He had his staff and things. Go now, go. He was out of the room now and in the hallway, emerald hallway. Greenlights, go. He went. Down the hallway.

Caleb descended to the lowest level in his charge. He stalked down the now-emerald corridor, from room to room, checking on the security of the occupants. He found they were all in place and safe as sardines, and the act of charging about, and of discharging his responsibilities, evacuated his mind of unwholesome humors. Wrapped in his role, he confirmed each silhouette was prepped in its space – each and every one – before marching to the far end of the first hall and sealing the exit portal. Next: the gas. At the top and bottom of the door, placed on opposite sides, and further apart than a man's wingspan could reach, were the access nodes. Both had to be activated at once to start the chemical flow; this was where the staff came into play. Laying the rod with the sensitive diodes athwart the heart of the gate, Caleb initiated the next stage in the process. Through the access panel, he saw the common spaces fill slowly with a yellow exhalation. Argon, he knew, was invisible, so he assumed that a colorant had been added to alert bystanders of its presence. The hallway clouded with a wispy, goldenrod essence, that thickened until it became a field of opaque mustard. He knew that the crawlspaces between the floors were flooded with the suppressant as well; only the habitations were kept secure.

Finishing the first floor was transformative. Caleb felt that he had served his purpose and now

needed only to manifest this persona over again –
and again and again – until the final iteration of
his function was complete. He did the next floor,
and then the floor above it as well. And then the
floor above that one as well. It was good. After
he had cocooned the idle occupants, he always
emptied the same strain of gas into an identical-
looking hallway. But he did his job faster now.
He improved. Knowing that there were other
Wardens working in the other Quadrants of the
Tower, Caleb agonized to pull ahead of them.
With no sacrifice of rigor, he applied a propulsion
to his efforts, rocketing steadily through the
floors of vacant occupants, sealing them
hermetically, and then fumigating their common
spaces. He did this and he did this and he did this.

And then, floors and floors above where he had
started, he came finally upon a floor lit in an
amber color. Not green? More of a straight
orange, actually – like the gas itself, but earthier…
He took a few cautious steps into his new
environment, uncertain. It was just another floor
of the Longshot building, much like any other,
but differently lit and it might as well have been
the surface of the moon. He trod deliberately,
tenderly, working his way towards the center of
the space. No one was there; it seemed not even
possible for a person to be there, the corridor was
so lifeless.

Caleb wanted to call out, but he knew there
would be no response; he had taken everyone he

knew and locked them away in a suffocating mist, and now he was here alone. Why was it so different? The lights blinked in the ceiling, forming a pattern that lead onward, calling on him to act, somehow.

And he remembered, then, that some of the floors would be simply empty. In fact, the rest of his whole column, straight to the top, was uninhabited and the change in lighting signaled that fact. This was the Desert. And since it was empty, there was no requirement to seal off the spaces between floors: the Learning told him that all he needed do was maneuver through the intervening levels, floating upward, until he made it to the final hatch. That tightly closed, the whole sector would be dosed at once. So he had to move. He had to get to high ground. Caleb got in motion, again.

In simulation of an actual fire, the elevators were all locked down and he was obliged to climb the stairs, serpentining back and forth along the halls until he reached the main landing, where he'd be able to take the corner staircase all the way up to the roof. He broke into a brisk trot, everything jiggling along with him; he had a long way to go. And he had to beat the other Wardens there, too. Chugging along through barren, no-longer-named places, Caleb thought orange thoughts about winning. His last victory had been ruined by earthquake and deluge, practically rained on, and he felt he deserved another, honestly he did. He picked up the pace a little, almost jogging now, and making his way up the stairs between floors with floating, fairy footsteps.

And the tangerine sameness lulled him. Threading slowly upward through the hollowed ziggurat, he could not sustain his focus on the prospect of a distant victory. Time passed. As he jiggled, he started thinking worthless, unorchestrated things, and asking himself worthless questions: if nothing rhymed with orange and the corridor was orange, was there a shape then that rhymed with the corridor? Or a color? He kept up his canter, tripping along the hallways in a blur of motion, until the emanation of his mind began to fade and tapered down to a tenuous line, and then ceased. His internal narrative was a blank. Limblessly, Caleb drifted forward and upward along straight lines and little curls. He became detached to the point where he was almost blind, almost smoke.

As the windstream carried him onward buoyantly, fear breathed again up behind. At first so subtle that it seemed just another exhalation, perhaps but poorly timed. He carried on in motion – for a space of time – but then it was upon him as a whisper, persistent at his back. Something was behind him. He knew it. Caleb felt a shapelessness inside his body that seemed to want to rise. He could not know what it was, but he wanted to outrun it, to outstrip it if he could.

He accelerated now, his knees rising. Maybe it was argon that pursued him. Maybe? Maybe it was an outbreak from one of the halls below? Maybe. Caleb still saw nothing or almost nothing; his neat, fleet little feet just carried him onward, but urgently now. He felt pockets of water form in his abdomen, clamoring panic and fear. Little vesicles that wanted to grow and would if he let them... Faster! He had to go faster! In a bid for speed – near desperate – he pumped his arms, up and down, riding the very rim of balance as he rounded the staircases. The ravenous charge of the unknown mounted behind him, gnashing up the space between in an implacable charge that bounds forward upon ribbons of muscle, twisted, corded. Its jaw, its maw is open and the slaver flows of an appetite insatiable, which seeks, which knows one thing only. Caleb is in sight! Paws, claws, and hooves all to the floor, all in the air – it is nigh upon him; his scent is filling its powerful head, his footfalls sound in its ears.

And Caleb is taken. Poor, scented prey, he topples like the helpless fawn; ignorant of all and only ever kind. Fear straddles him, horror hauls into him with long claws, pulling out from deep in his body the terrible sensations. Caleb's organs pulse and spasm; he is screaming. What is it? Get it off. Make it go away. Please. He rolls on the floor like a pill bug, opening and closing and turning all over, until finally coming to rest.

Caleb lay there for a while with his dry mouth

open, staring at the ceiling. The amber lights shone on, leading him forward. He rolled over and got his knees under him. He rested, with his head on the floor, panting heavily.

He rose. He put a shaky hand to his face; his face was wet. Caleb drew a kerchief from inside a vest pocket and dried himself. He was still quaking all over and his body wanted to sit. He did not know where he was – in a hallway, somewhere. There was a window at the far end. With dragging footsteps, Caleb drew himself in that direction, the staff trailing alongside and behind him.

Patches of the city, within the cloud cover, were visible to him. The buildings below came up like stubble through barren soil. He leaned heavily upon the glass and took deep breaths, gasping breaths, fighting back towards composure. It was over. Fear had passed into him, over him, through him, and now out of him, like a river poured forth from the breach of a dam, that runs a forceful current across unexpecting lands, but only once. And after the torrent, there was left only drying wreckage in the blare of the sun. The staff slipped from his grasp. Caleb lay his arms out wide so that his palms lay face-down on the sill, and then he pushed his rear leg back to make his shoulders bunch and his head hang at rest. It must have been about a quarter to noon.

Caleb straightened himself, then gave his face another press with the rag and devoted special attention to the hollows behind his jaw on both sides, right and left. He then held the fabric taut between his rigid fingers, halved it, quartered it, and laid it carefully away. He felt strong now, somehow, in a puny way, like a young plant that had bent before the storm and who now stood boldly upright, in fair weather. Whatever it was that had come up behind had overtaken him; it now lay far ahead, but perhaps not out of reach.

And he knew. Like an egg cracking, he suddenly knew. Vera lay ahead, before him, and he was in pursuit. Memory told him that she had not been in any of the spaces he had visited and Reason whispered in his ear that, since she did not have access to any other quarter of the building, there was nowhere else that she might be. With a flick, he took up his staff and made a pivot to face down the hall again. He came to the stairwell upward and stopped to indulge a moment of vanity, digging in his pocket for a gel that he rubbed precisely into his hair, and then gently touching his collar, buckle, and lapels to make sure they all were well.

He began his ascent at an easy pace, his footfalls counting the stairs. His speed was even, regular – how far ahead could Vera be? Perhaps quite far, but it would not matter; the path to the roof was long, quite long, and there was nowhere else to go. He could catch her. Caleb let the crank in his pelvis turn so that his piston legs rose and fell a beat the faster. He had time on his side – yes, time – and certainty, too. His feet pressed into the carpet as he crossed another hall, rose another floor, and laid on speed. Caleb rode forward along a hidden rail that drew him on, through a blurring mesh of amber spaces, faster and faster, and he did not tire. He felt young. The orange lamps in the halls were almost gold in his eye as he whipped through them; he had never been to this place before, but he knew he would not be lost. Forward was the only way, and upward with it too.

His urgent footfalls were silent on the gathered pile, and the fabric of his streaming clothing cracked and scraped like autumn. He was charging now, and the pump of his legs was hydraulic. For him, the body mechanism turned and churned, and the core temperature rose; heat roared through vents in his jacket. At the head of a shimmering wake he blew onto the landing, which had been shuttered into darkness and only the lights in the ceiling showed him the honey-trail forward. He cut a phosphorous hiss through the dark and an inner dynamo whined up to put the power to him; the air roared by in his ears. He would have her – oh he knew it, *how* he knew it – and time there would be enough.

He breached the final access tower: the lights inside were red. Caleb's breathed into his firm ascent, now more insistent, and more and more. There was a stroke to his legs, a stroke of pure-fuel conversion into fire, crackling energy.

Caleb's rise shimmered now as he made his assault on the final point. His hammerhead footfalls propelled him 'round the rising tower as his ascent riveted into the stairs. He was seamless: his garments were all high polymer.

> Lightning will shimmer over your bones –
> Know how subtle our strength is.

Caleb had energy without end, but the road was finite and the ultimate destination was at last at hand. In the final cycles of his rise, he became a device whose world was motion; motion was its purpose. The lights hummed at the low end of the spectrum. Staff in hand, he left the throttle to play and laid wide the intake ports to let radiation exhaust itself into the jet stream. And then, at last, with final force, Caleb made impact with the exit shield and blew through to the world outside.

And the sun was high in the sky. He came to a stop in the open space and a firm, even wind tagged the fabric of his pants, drawing them back behind him. The air was warm and pleasant. It was clear, too: his vision reached unimpeded into a sky of infinity blue.

He saw her. She was traveling along a line normal to the angle of his vision. She was a horrible, skittering mass; Caleb drew his arm back and held the staff, again, as a missile. She was distant, but he could reach her. He augured her acceleration, plotted the path she'd take along her panicked ray of flight, and loosed. His shining shiv glinted in the noontime glare on its parabola, ever a tangent to the curve described. He watched it. Caleb, for a puzzled second, could not tell if she was running forward to meet the projectile in its fall, or if it was diving towards her. It did not matter. The burning lance continued in its fated trajectory, ever-angling, until it terminated at a point of intersection beyond his view, where their lines fatefully crossed, behind a shed-like apparatus.

Caleb stood. He looked about him: the rooftop surface of the Longshot tower was a vast expanse. Here and there it was dotted with small structures. The sun was an eye above.

He walked towards the place where Vera had been; he did not feel much as he rounded the corner to come to the place where she might lie. His breast was empty. And he looked: she is there? She was gone. In the space where he expected her, his staff rocked instead, lazily working towards the edge. He stopped the thing with his toe and hiked his trousers before sinking to fetch it up. It surprised him that there was no guide or railing at the landing's outer lip, but there was none and the drop was sheer. Carefully, he stepped up and put his weight forward a little bit, just so he could peer downwards, straight down along the flank of the edifice. The whole urban space was before and below him, at such a distance that all he could see of it was its color and texture. The city looked like sand. Caleb stepped back again and looked to the right and to the left; Vera was not there. He walked back to the entrance through which he'd arrived at the rooftop and sealed it. Thus, he became the first Warden to complete this stage of the drill, which was an honor.

A couple minutes later, the next of the four Wardens came up. They met in the center of the flags and talked a little. Caleb found the conversation comforting, for the young man had the same basic ideas about the direction of the fashions and the times as Caleb did, and yet Caleb was a little saddened that his special status as First to Arrive was not remarked upon. Ultimately, the other two joined them and were just as pleasant under the high-overhead sun. Caleb's shadow was a tiny stain under his feet. The next step was for all of them to touch the ends of their staves together and, thereby, transmit the signal through the building that the recovery phase would soon initiate. This they did, and there were smiles all around. Then everyone went their separate ways.

The halls were lit in optic white when Caleb returned, and the elevators functioned again. He walked down the perfect hall – only moments ago evacuated of gas – to a sealed capsule, and he rode it down to the inhabited levels. He set everybody free. First he'd cycle the filtration systems and purify the air, then he'd enter the common hallways and release the captives' locks, one by one, to let them all return to their offices and finish up the day. He was struck again by how few people remained in the airy colossus that was Longshot: some of the floors held only one or two people. He gave Sophie a dignified nod as he opened up her chamber signaling that the path back to her workplace lay open. She nodded back in return. Caleb kept on his circuit until the last cell in the honeycomb had been uncapped and the final worker freed.

He rode the elevator down then. It was a very great plunge from his current height to the server rooms, deep underground, which would also need the argon driven from them. At the very start of his descent, Caleb experienced a whoopsie-moment of weightlessness, and then settled in for the ride down. There was no proper window in the elevator, just a narrow vertical slit a couple inches wide that ran from the ceiling to the floor. It was faced with transparent material and he looked at this so that he had something to focus on. The air in the elevator was warm. When the ribbon of light flashed black, Caleb knew he was underground. Fluorescent lighting ticked on. Upon deceleration, Caleb felt his body reengage with the complex mathematics of gravity, as a final, sobering weight.

When the doors opened, there was an abrupt thermal rush as the inner and the outer environments equalized. It was hot and Caleb could feel the heat in every crack in his skin. He started down the hall; it was like walking through a room with an open furnace roaring. And there was a roar, too, an indistinct static of industry, like iron-white noise.

Caleb came to the observation deck and looked into the wall of opaque vapor. The station used to initiate the final purification was there, and he activated it; once he could confirm that the hall was cleared, the drill would be over. When the engines started, he could barely hear them over the limitless sound like salt poured over a drumhead, which thronged his ears. Gradually the air began to thin, but it was slow happening. The heat. The heat came from the servers, the racks of computing equipment down below. And the sound, too. As the field of colored argon fell to a low mist, Caleb, from his eminence, watched a proud architecture emerge. Beneath and all around him, stretching into the distance, there was an expanse of senseless machinery, crackling with constant motion.

11

Vera had left the building and Caleb's job was done. He was to be fêted. Notice of an impending rendezvous to celebrate his success came as he sat at his desk, overseeing the girls. There were to be speeches, fine dining, entertainment, and an award of some sort. Such news! He was a good boy and he had done a good job and he deserved a cookie, yes he did. Certainly, he did. Caleb puffed like a balloon and spent the evening venting off blasts of hot and happy, happy, happy air until late in the night, as he lay in bed beside Sophie.

But the very next day when, shortly before the event was due to start, he received an automated notice from Human Resources telling him to clean out his desk, and his mood reversed. He felt black and awful. Had he been terminated? It did not clearly say… But he was to, immediately, vacate his place of work and remove any personal items. Caleb started up, back, and away from his station, but silently – somehow – so as not to attract attention to himself and his condition.

Could it be? At last?

There was no option but obedience. But

looking down at his desk, Caleb was struck by a strange realization: he appeared to own nothing. The workstation, the peripherals, and the furnishings were all Longshot property. There was a dynamic picture frame as well, which displayed images of his liking – with snappy transitions to boot – but it wasn't his. Even his tablet and stylus were company-provided. He put them on the desk. There didn't seem to be anything for him to remove from the workspace, but he could not simply do *nothing*; it felt non-compliant, somehow. Then, looking over the vacant desktop, which stood above his navel, he had an idea. Getting down on all fours, he lowered his workstation, bringing it back to its original height. Caleb dropped his seat down as well in a single, pneumatic motion, diminishing it. When he stood back up to look at the assembly, it seemed so puny; he absolutely dwarfed it all. But it looked like it could belong to someone else now – it was not his. Standing before the table, he bent over to put his full weight on his palms. He felt horrible, utterly lanced. Gutted. Just spit through and worthless. The picture frame showed him a cheery picture of a palm tree.

"Caleb, get your hands off my desk," came a voice behind him.

"Have I been fired?" he asked.

"Thank you," Old George replied, easily ignoring his question and responding instead to

Caleb's getting his buffed little fingers off the tabletop.

Caleb turned around to face the executive; even though he was much taller than the boss, looking down at him he felt cowed and tiny.

"Have I been let go? Should I be looking for work?"

"Caleb, my boy, come with me. I'm here to escort you to the big event!"

Caleb felt unimportant and uneasy. George directed him away from the office, after appropriate pleasantries with the staff, and then down various hallways. Caleb gloomed along behind him, just following the old man's lead. He was well-fed and old, but in no way decrepit; George's gait was charged, and he swung his arms about with purpose and power. Caleb felt stupid. At the end of the long and winding trek, George showed him into a changing room near the observation deck and instructed him to put on the formal attire that lay draped over a chair at the center of the chamber.

"I think you'll find the fit agreeable," George said. "One must look one's best for days such as these, you know. I'll be back when the time is right." And when might that be? George left, clicking the door closed behind him.

Caleb stood staring for a moment, then he stripped. His body was slim and shapely, trim and tanned and toned. Slowly, he picked up the separate pieces of the outfit and put them on, one by one. Now not even the cloth on his back was his. Did he own anything, really? Other than a stuffed goat and that uncharacterizable thing that Yoon had given him? Clothing, he supposed, and whatever food he bought before he ate it; after he ate it, it probably became the property of the shipping conglomerate that owned his stomach. He definitely didn't own any of the furniture in his apartment, since it had all been there when the company provided the domicile to him. His mind trailed hopelessly behind his thoughts, following them about, much as his physical person had followed George around, just now. He remembered things, little things mainly, like something he'd eaten for dinner once, and a time when he couldn't find a sock. Then he remembered –

> *At His quivering heart then You angle your spears*
> *And kindle His frame*
> *To make coals of his fame*
> *And a coke of His limbs and an ash of His years.*

It occurred to him that he was being celebrated, basically, because he had killed someone. Or, rather, that he had taken actions likely resulting in another person's death. He felt that he should probably feel bad about this; it was probably the thing to do.

The walls of the cell were gray, trimmed in white, and the floor was very stark. Caleb took a few steps, just to listen to his footfalls in the new shoes, and then he stopped to stare at the blank wall again. As a faint voice, he heard inside himself:

> Thus, in my vault
> Beneath the mystic weight of salt
> He comes as gentle snow – He falls;
> His ashes shimmer through my halls
> And in the deep.
> Soft as the moon He sinks at last, and soft as sleep.
> I embers gather, here and there,
> Plucking from the watr'y air,
> From coral bed and phosphorescent reef
> The simple cinders of His bones.
> How from its soul the Ocean moans –
> The crushing Water groans a black and crushing grief:
> He's lost. I cannot find Him now:
> My fist holds only earth.
> He's lost, as clover to the plow…
> My temple was His birth.

The colors were very faint now, almost washed out. He sat in the chair and waited for George to return. He sat under the white lights and waited.

George came back with a number of people whom Caleb did not recognize, though they all seemed very happy; George himself was ebullient and emotionally opaque at the same time – a jolly sort of cipher – and he helped Caleb eagerly out of his chair with every appearance of warm excitement.

"Come now, Caleb. It's time. They're waiting."

Caleb got up, his legs straightening. Following George and his coterie out, he was surprised that they did not simply make for the landing, but instead piled into an elevator, bound straight for the top. Caleb stood anxiously behind George; the old man's hair came to just under his nose, and the scent of his scalp cream was stannic and strong... Had Caleb been fired? He was still uncertain. When the elevator stopped, everyone got out and marched into the high, high hallway, the one that led straight to George's office.

And what a surprise awaited Caleb there! As they entered, the people who filled the office, which had been lined with chairs and staffed with bodies, rose as one and their applause was powerful, high-thundering. At the front, a pulpit was set before the crowd, somewhat elevated, and two towering portraits flanked it on either side, hanging from the ceiling. Caleb looked, and on one side was the likeness of the Founder, done in forceful lines and colors in the style of Tarot, and then on the other... himself? It was! Caleb's knees quivered as he saw his own profile, exquisitely rendered in gold and silver, turned to face that majestic image on an equal level. He staggered, grabbing at his satellites for support; the applause but rose the higher. Half-carried, he made his way to the frontmost rank of seats and was placed in a golden chair, as his head turned and lost itself in a solar glory.

George rose before them all and spoke. "Caleb's deeds were great," he proclaimed. "So, too, shall be his desserts." There was applause, then there was silence. "There is a method through all this, a way that leads forward, and Caleb has shown loyalty to the Founder's vision throughout. I ask you: does Longshot not show care for those who do well in its service?"

"Yes," chorused back the crowd.

"Are we not lavish here in gifts and praise, with those whose merits shine?"

"Yes." Again.

"And is he not our *golden boy*, who rose in our time of adversity, to come to the aid of this, our enterprise? Are we not fulsome in our recognition of achievement?"

"Yes," they all agreed. George's voice boomed forward, as if from an amplifying device; he stood totally still, robed in gleaming graphite.

"So we are!" he confirmed, with resonant confidence. "And now look on the rich reward he has earned so justly." Then the lights cut out, a video rolled, and Caleb beheld his compensation. It looked like he was going on a trip. A vacation! His reward was travel to a place far away, up north, in the land of the midnight sun. He beheld a panoramic view of a brave hotel, nestled in among the crags; hewn griffins guarded its doors, their forepaws lain upon massive nuggets of solid gold. Snow fell about it all, white as feathers, in inviting fluffy drifts. What skiing it promised!

"The skiing is simply the best," George continued. He praised the facility in all its details with effervescent adumbration. Then he bowed to the crowd, giving way to the next encomiast, and assumed his seat.

Caleb tingled now, all over, warm as sunshine. People ascended to the podium to speak, but it did not seem to matter much what they said: the image of their devotion alone gave him satisfaction enough. They were praising him. He felt the warmth in the room, such a warmth, and that strange smell he'd first noticed up here long ago was very pronounced – sort of smoky and metallic. The orators rotated and the eulogies kept coming. Caleb felt he knew exactly what would happen: this would not be like the time he won that tiny award for that meager scrap of advertising he had done. This would be bigger, would be better, and would go off smoothly. He felt another tug at something – his feelings or his conscience – over the way in which Vera had exited the building, but he comforted himself. After all, the elevators to the ground floor had been out of order, so no one could go down to confirm that she had landed. It was possible that she was fine. Maybe she had escaped somehow? Maybe she just went away. Caleb took refuge in the fact that anything might have happened.

When it came to be his turn to speak, he kept his address simple. Caleb thanked the crowd, praised the Founder for his vision, gave due credit to George for his leadership, and then he spoke the lines:

> Happiness shines from on high
> > And Virtue grows warm in the morning;
> Peace in the tower, come at long last –
> > Tranquil, even, and graceful.
>
> Who ever doubted our way?
> > And who could so blindly remain now?

The results were as positive as if it had been ordained that they should be so. Afterwards, there was a meal. Caleb sat alongside George, who watched him eagerly take every bite, as if he were tasting Caleb's succulent repast himself. And Caleb cleaned his plate.

That night, when he got home, he found that his few genuinely personal items were gone. Sophie had always insisted on a strict division of their shared space, and his side was as stark and bare as if the bark had been stripped clean off it.

"Where are my things?" he asked her.

"Oh, they're gone. Sent forward."

"Sent where?"

"To the hotel. It actually seemed pretty convenient to me; you won't need to deal with any of the fuss or headache yourself."

"But who did this? Who took my things?"

Sophie looked at him as if this was a really dumb question to ask.

"Well, what will I wear tomorrow? I can't just walk around with the same old clothes on again."

"I'm certain they've made preparations. I'm certain everything will be fine."

Caleb missed his stuffed goat and it wasn't fair that it was gone. That night, he dreamt that he was a bird, perched on the ramparts of Longshot, and that he took flight. The air held him aloft; he skated forward on transparent feathers. But then he fell. Caleb's line of sight angled downward and he looked full into the terrifying face of the earth. His muscles pulsed and he tried to change his situation. He tried to fight. It did not matter – his fate was sure as Microinsurance. The wind beat terribly against his eyes, his ears, his hopeless, broken wings. It did not matter at all. His vision narrowed, perspective changed, and then there was a horrible, unambiguous moment of resolution.

He sat bolt upright. In bed. Awake. Wide awake. Drenched. Caleb was flowing with perspiration. Oh no, he'd wet the bed! No, he hadn't. He'd just… his heart was racing.

A couple of pre-packaged sets of clothes were delivered the next morning. And, thereafter, Caleb had time. There was still a short gap between his recognition and the final receipt of his reward, but his responsibilities had been nullified. For the remainder of the pay period, he was free. Caleb walked the halls, his own man, a hopeless mess. He still didn't really know if he had a job or not; the reward had come with a bunch of free Microinsurance policies, but he was too scared to try applying for unemployment coverage. They'd let him keep his accesses, so he was able to wander freely about the building. Sophie remained pinned to her desk, generating product, so Caleb was alone. He took long walks on idle circuits.

Caleb had only two skills, really, and those were graphic design and management. No longer able to produce images, he spent his hours among the unoccupied Longshot honeycombs, supervising the structure. The complexity of interlacing systems fascinated him. He looked into a toilet somewhere and tried to imagine the capillary of bronze at its base kinking backward to empty into a larger vein somewhere hidden, which would mate further on with a broader artery, emptying itself, and then that artery would evacuate its own contents into a great aorta of waste in a location probably very far beneath his feet, completing and initiating some sort of cycle. Pondering this magnitude and complexity, Caleb began to find the building's waste disposal facilities menacing – both in the perfection of their design and their omnipresence. Agents of the temperature control system hung over him, from around every corner.

He was investigating an element of the

electrical apparatus, when he began to suspect that he'd returned to the place where Vera had bitten him. It was just a feeling. The lighting was different and both the carpeting and the paint-job had been redone. Caleb remembered how she had scrawled murals across the walls, rioting color up and down on every side. He gazed closely at the new, taupe surface, trying to discern a hidden substrate, and passed his sensitive fingers over the surface of the dry topcoat. Nothing. But, then again, he was not even sure that this was the same place and, the next day, he couldn't even find his way back.

And then the time of his departure arrived, rather abruptly. Caleb had been on the lowest observation desk, staring flat out into the bronze horizon of morning, when he heard the PA system click on behind him. He trotted back inside to see what the news was.

"Please join me this afternoon," Old George announced, "for the great *bon voyage* of our own hero, so recently crowned. He will be saying goodbye to all of us, so attendance is expected and leave will be granted for the event."

The finality of his words was troubling, like a bell that was being struck in a spire. Caleb felt a powerful urge to see Sophie, and his bowels trembled as if this might be the last thing he would ever do. He rushed. Caleb ran up stairs, down hallways, and took elevators to close the distance between himself and her. He ran as if a solar mass bore down upon his body from behind, and the path he trod collapsed in fragile ash behind him.

Just before turning the corner to the office, Caleb poised to collect himself. He panted until his breath was a presentable metronome and then he regulated the rest of his body so that it would be presentable. To her. It seemed dreadfully important right now, though he could not quite articulate why. He checked his whole person, up and down, for imperfections; he saw his own face staring back at him, in the shine of his Longshot-provided shoes. Then he rounded the corner and walked straight into a pair of men who were waiting there for him.

"Hello, Caleb," they said. "We've been waiting for you. Are you ready for your photos?"

"Yes," he said, reflexively cooperative. "I am. May I...?" and he made a motion towards the office door, behind which was Sophie.

"You can come with us," they said. Their tone reminded Caleb of George telling him to get his hands off his desk.

"But I've got to..." and he motioned again. "It's really quite important. See? I've got to make an impression on them, my workers, right now, or it will all be lost. My people. They need to know... They need to know how much they mattered and how great their role was – with me. I need to see them. It won't take long? This is important."

Caleb felt himself trying to be the Manager one final time; he did not mention Sophie.

"That is well. They will be notified," came the response. "You can come with us."

And Caleb went with them. He spent the hours intervening between his pick-up and the moment of departure posing for promotional photos, showcasing the fun he would be having way up north, where the sun never sets. He pretend-slalomed down slopes carpeted in goose down and tanned himself under artificial skies, while shutters flattered him. Pliant was Caleb in this setting – pliant and capable and kind. The photographer didn't seem to want much, just that he put his limbs here and here and tilt his face so… but he felt that horrible demands were being exacted from him, as he crouched like a puma with sunbathing gear on. The pattern on the towel was stupid, but he posed there and time passed. And he did not know why he did this, why he complied.

Finally, they were satisfied – a good thing too, for his haunches were sore and the Big Goodbye was about to start. They hurried him first into his clothes and then up to the building's roof. Caleb had dressed so quickly that he was worried he had put his underwear on backwards as he staggered weakly onto the scene of Vera's probable demise, his pelvis thrown off balance. People were there. The transportation, a helicopter, huddled in readiness at center stage with its blade spinning. George came out to receive him in the turbulence with his hair cast all on end.

"Y'see?" he said, forcing his voice to be heard above the motor's roar as he pointed to twin banners, floating above. On them was written:

Greatness will beacon over the land –
Burning, shimmering brightly.

"That's for you!" he called, barely audible over the beating of the whirling blades. Gesturing to the crowd, he commanded, "Wave to them!"

Looking out over the small clot of gathered persons, Caleb made a big-arm motion. Sophie might have been out there, but he didn't see her. Mona probably was, too. It had bothered him at a very deep level that he had not been able to take his lady with him at first, but now he was resigned to it: the success was his, and it was only fair to the other employees that those not directly involved in his achievements did not derive a benefit. It was just and it was proper.

Caleb gripped the runner by the portal to the cabin, turned, and made another big-arm motion. Very big. The crowd might have cheered. Then he felt the upward tug of the craft and knew that he was airborne. He did not feel light; he felt heavy and dragged free of the earth. As the machine angled away and the tower of Longshot became a hulking silhouette amid the cityscape, he saw the sun's light lancing down, as radiance.

> *I embers gather, here and there,*
> *Plucking from the watr'y air,*
> *From coral bed and phosphorescent reef*
> *The simple cinders of His bones.*
> *But from its soul the Ocean moans,*
> *The crushing Water groans a black, unending grief:*
>
> *He's lost. I cannot find Him now:*
> *My fist holds only earth.*
> *He's lost, as clover to the plow –*
> *My temple was his birth.*

He stared at the ground, far below. The conveyance went north. Caleb had left the building.

THE POEMS
COMPOSED

DIONYSIAN DITHYRAMB

I.

We strut beneath the wave and dance on sand
      Earth rising where we stand;
    Fish titter as we pace,
    And coral part apace
      Shrinking at His command,
  As on we go. The marlin gapes
In worship as he sees our forms, our shapes
  Incise, cut through the waving drapes
Of seaweed on the ocean floor.
Above, the basking seals roar,
The otters keen, upon the shore.
    "Your goading wounds the sea will tend...
     "O, Grace to Man,
     "O, Grace to Man,
  "Your bones will knit, His flesh will mend."

Chorus

"Your goading wounds the sea will tend...
    "O, Grace to Man,
    "O, Grace to Man,
"Your bones will knit, His flesh will mend."

II.

His heart pounds in the dark
    And footsteps through His veins.
    The fiber of His tendons strains:
He plants His limbs, He takes His mark
                  And on the sky He trains
His eyes. I *hear* Him rise.
His pulses drumming up the skies –
The sea sounds back. The salt replies.
And with His surging all the creatures dance:
The rays join hands, seahorses prance;
    The shark, the herring, and the hake
    Combine to decorate His wake
In chorus, through the thinning sea
A great procession sun-ward swings, and in its van is He
Alone. The tattoo of His chambered heart
Leads fin to gill in one ecstatic Art.
It's shallow now. He breaches from the school! They
part.
         Old Ocean rides
         Upon all sides
         Of that small reach
         Upon the beach
   Where He stands in the tides.

           Chorus

         Old Ocean rides
         Upon all sides
         Of that small reach
         Upon the beach
   Where He stands in the tides.

III.

His eyes take in the sun that dominates the air
    In this, which is an arid land and bare.
        The sands beneath those rays flash white
        And radiate their solar might
           Into His marine face
           As he begins to pace
Inland. His steaming tracks His will declare:
    "This! Which is an arid land and bare,
        "My sacrament will soon proclaim!
    "The buried seed will turn to grow,
    "The spring long lost begin to flow.
        "The seed to grow!
        "The spring to flow!
    "*Life* again will know its name."

Chorus

"The buried seed will turn to grow,
"The spring long lost begin to flow.
"The seed to grow!
"The spring to flow!
*"*Life *again will know its name."*

IV.

    The infant green starts from its bed
        At once; the curling tendrils spread
Across the waste, in sympathetic echo at His tread,
           Much as the river mounts its dam:
           The waters white, first, as the lamb,
           As froth, as lace; but then the flood -
           That roaring *excess* of the blood -

Erupting from the breach
As vines and trees and grasses each
Effuse to claim the lifeless land.
All sprout and branch and strain,
Rising, rising, rising, rising,
Rising from the unmarked plain
To fruit and shade the sand.

Creatures, emerging from the green,
Dart and repose, seen and unseen;
The lion, boar, the ugly ram,
And then the lamb – You are the Lamb.

You gambol near, seek cover from the rain.
His eyes are mad. His breath is warm.
He parts your skin and reaches in.
You give – the sapling in the storm,
The gasping votive to His sin.

Chorus

His eyes are mad. His breath is warm.
He parts your skin and reaches in.
You give – the sapling in the storm,
The gasping votive to His sin.

V.

About the tender body rise
Such trees as flower to the skies,
That shadows scatter. O, young leaf –
Who to the flock provides relief –
Wither now! *You* cook His veins,
Sear him white 'til ash remains.
Dominate! You are the *Sun*.
Bake the hills! Where rivers run

Vapor only carries now.
Boil the cloud! Prevent the rains!
Drive the sunbeam as the plow!
Green recedes; bright stone now gains…
Devastate and cauterize –
Blast the plain that 'round him lies.

Gold-shining in your light, the cities mount,
All full of spires, full of men who count.
About Him, now, your flames advance and grow
Pain lines His brow
Who, shifting now,
Did turn and run, turn and run,
Turn and run and, turning, show
That though He sought to flee th' advancing Sun,
Your holocaust consumes the world as One.

Chorus

About Him now your flames advance and grow
Pain lines His brow
Who, shifting now,
Did turn and run, turn and run,
Turn and run and, turning, show
That though He sought to flee th' advancing Sun,
Your holocaust consumes the world as One.

VI.

His feet but dot the frying sands
As faster yet – and faster yet – His hands
Scythe through the sparking grasses. See
How His divine, unhing'd velocity
Far, *far* Him drives in rout.

His smoke's in the air
Your flame's in His hair
And – panicked – His wind gives out.
Revenge, revenge pours from the skies!
Iron columns arise!
Molten beams down you cast,
Sterilizing in your blast
All the pastures, as your rays incise
Deep in the land. Advance!
Stop His song! End the dance!
Drive Him from the earth, then crucible the seas –
And heed you not his pleas –
But run Him to His knees;
With His final moans,
Burn Him in His bones.

Behold Him now trudge the surf-foam; He fears
As the vapors rise under your gaze
And scald into air at your masculine blaze.
The seabed's lain bare and the moment now nears:
At His quivering heart then you angle your spears
And kindle His frame
To make coals of His fame
And a coke of His limbs, and an ash of His years.

Chorus

At His quivering heart then you angle your spears
And kindle His frame
To make coals of His fame
And a coke of His limbs, and an ash of His years.

VII.

       Thus, in my vault
Beneath the mystic weight of salt
       He comes as gentle snow – he falls;
His ashes shimmer through my halls
          And in the deep.
Soft as the moon he sinks at last, and soft as sleep.
    I embers gather, here and there,
     Plucking from the watr'y air,
From coral bed and phosphorescent reef
         The simple cinders of His bones.
         How from its soul the Ocean moans –
The crushing Water groans a black, unending grief:
      He's lost. I cannot find Him now:
        My fist holds only earth.
      He's lost, as clover to the plow…
        My temple was His birth.

Grand Chorus

    I embers gather, here and there,
     Plucking from the watr'y air,
From coral bed and phosphorescent reef
         The simple cinders of His bones.
         But from its soul the Ocean moans,
The crushing Water groans a black, unending grief:
      He's lost. I cannot find Him now:
        My fist holds only earth.
      He's lost, as clover to the plow…
        My temple was His birth.

APOLLONIAN HEXAMETER

High though the sky is and wide,
　　It's ours for today and tomorrow.
We will deliver, come storm and wind;
　　Raindrops, numbered and counted.

Fear not the seas or the wastes,
　　For certain there is a way onward.
Higher and higher, strain for the sun:
　　Father, giver of glory.

Hark to the times and give ear:
　　Oh, look to the Order that's written...
Now is it good and ever shall last –
　　Buckle, fall, and be humble.

I was the sign of bright day.
　　My works all shined forth through the cloud.
I was a golden line of bright light.
　　I burned signs across ages.

We will not stand in the shade;
　　Our force will command, overpower.
Heat waves will shimmer over your bones –
　　Know how subtle our strength is.

Happiness shines from on high,
    And Virtue grows warm in the morning
Peace in the tower come at long last –
    Tranquil, even, and graceful.

Who ever doubted our way?
    And who could so blindly remain now?
Greatness will beacon over the land,
    Burning, shimmering brightly.

ACKNOWLEDGMENTS

Euripides, pseudo-Homer, Walter F. Otto, Aristeas of Proconnesus, Friedrich Nietzsche, John Edwin Sandys, E. R. Dodds, William James, Callimachus, John Dryden, Samuel Taylor Coleridge, Pindar, Jane Ellen Harrison, and Lewis Richard Farnell.

Also...

Jessie, for staying with me (and being smart about things, too; Corbin and Hsin-Lun, for being my path home; Dad, for the free housing; Jonathan "Banjotan" Wichmann, for crawling out of the woodwork; Charles Petersen, for the dumb, simple advice I needed, right when I needed it; Steven Hill and Feng Chuan, for teaching me a thing or two about writing; Scott Carpenter, who would be surprised; all the minds of Sisu, for their understanding, support, and patience; the Federal Government, for not noticing my occasional abuse of its printing resources; Tom Haines, who kept up the fire, but did not fire me; Peep and all the language crew, for their kindness and stoic endurance of my work habits; the Voorhees family writ large, because their art and hospitality must be remembered; my Aunt Chickie and Uncle John, whose house I was in when I got the news that my labor of three and a half years would see the light of day; Dana Carrington, as the emergence of an ally in the final hour should ever be remembered; and Miette Gillette, the noble, immortal Publisher, with her pigs...

...but most of all I must acknowledge my poor mother, who will never know this book was published. Without her, I would never have started down this strange and winding path...

ABOUT THE AUTHOR

Maxwell Massa spent five years in China (including a year-long stint as a Mandarin TV star), only to return to the U.S. and find that — surprise! — intellectualism isn't really a thing here.

ABOUT THE PUBLISHER

Whisk(e)y Tit is committed to restoring degradation and degeneracy to the literary arts. We work with authors who are unwilling to sacrifice intellectual rigor, unrelenting playfulness, and visual beauty in our literary pursuits, often leading to texts that would otherwise be abandoned in today's largely homogenized literary landscape. In a world governed by idiocy, our commitment to these principles is an act of civil service and civil disobedience alike.